# Annihilation of Caste and Other Essays

*B.R. Ambedkar*



maple press

ANNIHILATION OF CASTE AND OTHER ESSAYS *by* B.R. Ambedkar



Published by

maple press

MAPLE PRESS PRIVATE LIMITED
office: A-63, Sector 58, Noida 201301, U.P., India
phone: +91 120 455 3581, 455 3583
email: info@maplepress.co.in
website: www.maplepress.co.in

Printed in 2026
India

ISBN: 978-93-90602-04-9

14 13 12 11 10 9 8 7 6

# Contents

# Annihilation of Caste

# Prologue

On 12 December 1935, I received the following letter from Mr. Sant Ram, the Secretary of the Jat-Pat Todak Mandal:

My dear Doctor Saheb,

Many thanks for your kind letter of the 5th December. I have released it for press without your permission, for which I beg your pardon, as I saw no harm in giving it publicity. You are a great thinker, and it is my well-considered opinion that none else has studied the problem of caste so deeply as you have. I have always benefited myself and our Mandal from your ideas. I have explained and preached it in the *Kranti* many times, and I have even lectured on it in many conferences. I am now very anxious to read the exposition of your new formula – "It is not possible to break caste without annihilating the religious notions on which it, the caste system, is founded." Please do explain it at length at your earliest convenience, so that we may take up the idea and emphasise it from press and platform. At present, it is not fully clear to me.

Our executive committee persists in having you as our president for our annual conference. We can change our dates to accommodate your convenience. Independent Harijans of Punjab are very much desirous to meet you and discuss with you their plans. So if you kindly accept our request and come to Lahore to preside over the conference, it will serve a double purpose. We will invite the Harijan leaders of all shades of opinion, and you will get an opportunity of giving your ideas to them.

The Mandal has deputed our Assistant Secretary, Mr. Indra Singh, to meet you at Bombay in Xmas and discuss with you the whole situation with a view to persuade you to please accept our request.

The Jat-Pat Todak Mandal is, I was given to understand, an organisation of caste-Hindu social reformers, with the one and only aim, namely, to eradicate the caste system from amongst the

Hindus. As a rule, I do not like to take any part in a movement which is carried on by caste Hindus. Their attitude towards social reform is so different from mine that I have found it difficult to pull on with them. Indeed, I find their company quite uncongenial to me on account of our differences of opinion. Therefore, when the Mandal first approached me, I declined their invitation to preside. The Mandal, however, would not take a refusal from me and sent down one of its members to Bombay to press me to accept the invitation. In the end, I agreed to preside. The annual conference was to be held at Lahore, the headquarters of the Mandal. The conference was to meet at Easter, but was subsequently postponed to the middle of May 1936.

The reception committee of the Mandal has now cancelled the conference. The notice of cancellation came long after my presidential address had been printed. The copies of this address are now lying with me. As I did not get an opportunity to deliver the address from the presidential chair, the public has not had an opportunity to know my views on the problems created by the caste system.

To let the public know them and also to dispose of the printed copies which are lying on my hand, I have decided to put the printed copies of the address in the market. The accompanying pages contain the text of that address.

The public will be curious to know what led to the cancellation of my appointment as the president of the conference. At the start, a dispute arose over the printing of the address. I desired that the address should be printed in Bombay. The Mandal wished that it should be printed in Lahore, on the grounds of economy. I did not agree and insisted upon having it printed in Bombay. Instead of their agreeing to my proposition, I received a letter signed by several members of the Mandal, from which I give the following extract:

27 March 1936

Revered Doctorji,

Your letter of the 24th instant addressed to Sjt Sant Ram has been shown to us. We were a little disappointed to read it. Perhaps you are not fully aware of the situation that has arisen here. Almost all the Hindus in the Punjab are against your being invited to this province. The Jat-Pat Todak Mandal has been subjected to the bitterest criticism and has received censorious rebuke from all quarters. All the Hindu leaders, among whom being Bhai Parmanand, MLA (ex-president, Hindu Mahasabha), Mahatma Hans Raj, Dr. Gokal Chand Narang, Minister for local self-government, Raja Narendra Nath, MLC, etc., have dissociated themselves from this step of the Mandal.

Despite all this, the runners of the Jat-Pat Todak Mandal (the leading figure being Sjt Sant Ram) are determined to wade through thick and thin but would not give up the idea of your presidentship. The Mandal has earned a bad name.

Under the circumstances, it becomes your duty to co-operate with the Mandal. On the one hand, they are being put to so much trouble and hardship by the Hindus, and if, on the other hand, you, too, augment their difficulties, it will be a most sad coincidence of bad luck for them.

We hope you will think over the matter and do what is good for us all.

This letter puzzled me greatly. I could not understand why the Mandal should displease me, for the sake of a few rupees, in the matter of printing the address. Secondly, I could not believe that men like Sir Gokal Chand Narang had really resigned as a protest against my selection as president, because I had received the following letter from Sir Gokal Chand himself:

5 Montgomery Road, Lahore

7 February 1936

Dear Doctor Ambedkar,

I am glad to learn from the workers of the Jat-Pat Todak Mandal that you have agreed to preside at their next anniversary to be held at Lahore during the Easter holidays. It will give me much pleasure if you stay with me while you are at Lahore.

More when we meet.

Yours sincerely,

G.C. Narang

Whatever be the truth, I did not yield to this pressure. But even when the Mandal found that I was insisting upon having my address printed in Bombay, instead of agreeing to my proposal, the Mandal sent me a wire that they were sending Mr. Har Bhagwan to Bombay to "talk over matters personally." Mr. Har Bhagwan came to Bombay on the 9th of April. When I met Mr. Har Bhagwan, I found that he had nothing to say regarding the issue. Indeed, he was so unconcerned regarding the printing of the address – whether it should be printed in Bombay or in Lahore – that he did not even mention it in the course of our conversation.

All that he was anxious for was to know the contents of the address. I was then convinced that in getting the address printed in Lahore, the main object of the Mandal was not to save money but to get at the contents of the address. I gave him a copy. He did not feel very happy with some parts of it. He returned to Lahore. From Lahore, he wrote to me the following letter:

Lahore, 14 April 1936

My Dear Doctor Saheb,

Since my arrival from Bombay on the 12th, I have been indisposed owing to my having not slept continuously for five or six nights, which were spent in the train. Reaching here, I came to know that you had come to Amritsar. I would have seen you there if I were well enough to go about. I have made over your address to Mr. Sant Ram for translation, and he has liked it very much, but he is not sure whether it could be translated by him for printing before the 25th. In any case, it would have a wide publicity, and we are sure it would wake the Hindus up from their slumber.

The passage I pointed out to you at Bombay has been read by some of our friends with a little misgiving, and those of us who would like to see the conference terminate without any untoward incident would prefer that at least the word "Veda" be left out for the time being. I leave this to your good sense. I hope, however, in your concluding paragraphs, you will make it clear that the views expressed in the address are your own and that the responsibility does not lie on the Mandal.

I hope you will not mind this statement of mine and would let us have 1,000 copies of the address, for which we shall, of course, pay. To this effect, I have sent you a telegram today. A cheque of

Rs 100 is enclosed herewith, which kindly acknowledge, and send us your bills in due time.

I have called a meeting of the reception committee and shall communicate their decision to you immediately. In the meantime, kindly accept my heartfelt thanks for the kindness shown to me and the great pains taken by you in the preparation of your address. You have really put us under a heavy debt of gratitude.

Yours sincerely,
Har Bhagwan

P.S.: Kindly send the copies of the address by passenger train as soon as it is printed, so that copies may be sent to the press for publication.

Accordingly, I handed over my manuscript to the printer with an order to print a thousand copies.

Eight days later, I received another letter from Mr. Har Bhagwan, which I reproduce below:

Lahore, 22 April 1936

Dear Dr. Ambedkar,

We are in receipt of your telegram and letter, for which kindly accept our thanks. In accordance with your desire, we have again postponed our conference, but feel that it would have been much better to have it on the 25th and 26th, as the weather is growing warmer and warmer every day in the Punjab. In the middle of May, it would be fairly hot, and the sittings in the daytime would not be very pleasant and comfortable. However, we shall try our best to do all we can to make things as comfortable as possible, if it is held in the middle of May.

There is, however, one thing that we have been compelled to bring to your kind attention. You will remember that when I pointed out to you the misgivings entertained by some of our people regarding your declaration on the subject of change of religion, you told me that it was undoubtedly outside the scope of the Mandal and that you had no intention to say anything from our platform in that connection. At the same time, when the manuscript of your address was handed to me, you assured me that that was the main portion of your address and that there were only two or three concluding paragraphs that you wanted to add. On receipt of the second instalment of your address, we have been taken by surprise, as that would make it so lengthy that we are afraid very few people would read the whole of it. Besides that, you have more than once stated in your address that you had decided to walk out of the fold of the Hindus and that that was your last address as a Hindu. You have also unnecessarily attacked the morality and reasonableness of the Vedas and other religious books of the Hindus and have at length dwelt upon the technical side of Hindu religion, which has absolutely no connection with the problem at issue, so much so that some of the passages have become irrelevant and off the point.

We would have been very pleased if you had confined your address to that portion given to me, or if an addition was necessary, it would have been limited to what you had written on Brahminism, etc. The last portion, which deals with the complete annihilation of the Hindu religion and doubts the morality of the sacred books of the Hindus, as well as a hint about your intention to leave the Hindu fold, does not seem to me to be relevant.

I would therefore most humbly request you, on behalf of the people responsible for the conference, to leave out the passages referred to above and close the address with what was given to me or add a few paragraphs on Brahminism. We doubt the wisdom of making the address unnecessarily provocative and pinching. There are several of us who subscribe to your feelings and would very much want to be under your banner for remodelling the Hindu religion. If you had decided to get together persons of your cult, I can assure you a large number would have joined your army of reformers from the Punjab.

In fact, we thought you would give us a lead in the destruction of the evil of the caste system, especially when you have studied the subject so thoroughly, and strengthen our hands by bringing about a revolution and making yourself as a nucleus in the gigantic effort, but a declaration of the nature made by you, when repeated, loses its power and becomes a hackneyed term. Under the circumstances, I would request you to consider the whole matter and make your address more effective by saying that you would be glad to take a leading part in the destruction of the caste system if the Hindus are willing to work in right earnest towards that end, even if they had to forsake their kith and kin and the religious notions. In case you do so, I am sanguine that you would find a ready response from the Punjab in such an endeavour.

I shall be grateful if you will help us at this juncture, as we have already undergone much expenditure and have been put to suspense, and let us know by the return of post that you have condescended to limit your address as above. In case you still insist upon the printing of the address *in toto*, we very much regret it would not be possible – rather advisable – for us to hold the conference, and would prefer to postpone it *sine die*, although by doing so we shall be losing the goodwill of the people because of the repeated postponements.

We should, however, like to point out that you have carved a niche in our hearts by writing such a wonderful treatise on the caste system, which excels all other treatises so far written and will prove to be a valuable heritage, so to say. We shall be ever indebted to you for the pains taken by you in its preparation.

Thanking you very much for your kindness and with best wishes.

I am yours sincerely,
Har Bhagwan

**To this letter, I sent the following reply:**

27 April 1936

Dear Mr. Har Bhagwan,

I am in receipt of your letter of the 22nd April. I note with regret that the reception committee of the Jat-Pat Todak Mandal "would prefer to postpone the conference *sine die*" if I insisted upon printing the address *in toto*.

In reply, I have to inform you that I also would prefer to have the conference cancelled – I do not like to use vague terms – if the Mandal insisted upon having my address pruned to suit its circumstances. You may not like my decision. But I cannot give up, for the sake of the honour of presiding over the conference, the liberty which every president must have in the preparation of the address. I cannot give up, for the sake of pleasing the Mandal, the duty which every president owes to the conference over which he presides, to give it a lead which he thinks right and proper. The issue is one of principle, and I feel I must do nothing to compromise it in any way.

I would not have entered into any controversy as regards the propriety of the decision taken by the reception committee. But as you have given certain reasons which appear to throw the blame on me, I am bound to answer them.

In the first place, I must dispel the notion that the views contained in that part of the address to which objection has been taken by the committee have come to the Mandal as a surprise. Mr. Sant Ram, I am sure, will bear me out when I say that in reply to one of his letters I had said that the real method of breaking up the caste system was not to bring about inter-caste dinners and inter-caste marriages but to destroy the religious notions on which caste was founded and that Mr. Sant Ram, in return, asked me to explain what he said was a novel point of view. It was in response to this invitation from Mr. Sant Ram that I thought I ought to elaborate in my address what I had stated in a sentence in my letter to him. You cannot, therefore, say that the views expressed are new. At any rate, they are not new to Mr. Sant Ram, who is the moving spirit and the leading light of your Mandal.

But I go further and say that I wrote this part of my address not merely because I felt it desirable to do so. I wrote it because I thought that it was absolutely necessary to complete the argument. I am amazed to read that you characterise the portion of the speech to which your committee objects as "irrelevant and off the point." You will allow me to say that I am a lawyer, and I know the rules of relevancy as well as any member of your committee. I most emphatically maintain that the portion objected to is not only most relevant but is also most important. It is in that part of the address that I have discussed the ways and means of breaking up the caste system. It may be that the conclusion I have arrived at as to the best method of destroying caste is startling and painful. You are entitled to say that my analysis is wrong. But you cannot say that in an address which deals with the problem of caste, it is not open to me to discuss how caste can be destroyed.

Your other complaint relates to the length of the address. I have pleaded guilty to the charge in the address itself. But who is really responsible for this? I fear you have come rather late on the scene. Otherwise, you would have known that originally I had planned to write a short address, for my own convenience, as I had neither the time nor the energy to engage myself in the preparation of an elaborate thesis. It was the Mandal which asked me to deal with the subject exhaustively, and it was the Mandal which sent down to me a list of questions relating to the caste system and asked me to answer them in the body of my address, as they were questions which were often raised in the controversy between the Mandal and its opponents and which the Mandal found difficult to answer satisfactorily. It was in trying to meet the wishes of the Mandal in this respect that the address has grown to the length to which it has. In view of what I have said, I am sure you will agree that the fault respecting the length of the address is not mine.

I did not expect that your Mandal would be so upset because I have spoken of the destruction of the Hindu religion. I thought it was only fools who were afraid of words. But lest there should be any misapprehension in the minds of the people, I have taken great pains to explain what I mean by religion and destruction of religion. I am sure that nobody, on reading my address, could possibly misunderstand me. That your Mandal should have taken a fright at mere words as "destruction of religion, etc.," notwithstanding the explanation that accompanies them, does not raise the Mandal in my estimation. One cannot have any respect or regard for men who take the position of the reformer and then refuse even to see the logical consequences of that position, let alone follow them out in action.

You will agree that I have never accepted to be limited in any way in the preparation of my address, and the question as to what the address should or should not contain was never even discussed between myself and the Mandal. I had always taken for granted that I was free to express in the address such views as I held on the subject. Indeed, until you came to Bombay on the 9th April, the Mandal did not know what sort of an address I was preparing. It was when you came to Bombay that I voluntarily told you that I had no desire to use your platform from which to advocate my views regarding the change of religion by the Depressed Classes. I think I have scrupulously kept that promise in the preparation of the address.

Beyond a passing reference to an indirect character where I say that "I am sorry I will not be here, etc.," I have said nothing about the subject in my address. When I see you object even to such a passing and so indirect a reference, I feel bound to ask, did you think that in agreeing to preside over your conference, I would be agreeing to suspend or to give up my views regarding change of faith by the Depressed Classes? If you did think so, I must tell you that I am in no way responsible for such a mistake on your part. If any of you had even hinted to me that in exchange for the honour you were doing me by electing me as president, I was to abjure my faith in my programme of conversion, I would have told you in quite plain terms that I cared more for my faith than for any honour from you.

After your letter of the 14th, this letter of yours comes as a surprise to me. I am sure that anyone who reads them both will feel the same. I cannot account for this sudden volte-face on the part of the reception committee. There is no difference in substance between the rough draft, which was before the committee when you wrote your letter of the 14th, and the final draft on which the decision of the committee communicated to me in your letter under reply was taken. You cannot point out a single new idea in the final draft which is not contained in the earlier draft. The ideas are the same. The only difference is that they have been worked out in greater detail in the final draft. If there was anything to object to in the address, you could have said so on the 14th. But you did not.

On the contrary, you asked me to print off 1,000 copies, leaving me the liberty to accept or not the verbal changes which you suggested. Accordingly, I got 1,000 copies printed, which are now lying with me. Eight days later, you write to say that you object to the address and that if it is not amended, the conference will be cancelled. You ought to have known that there was no hope of any alteration being made in the address. I told you when you were in Bombay that I would not alter a comma, that I would not allow any censorship over my address and that you would have to accept the address as it came from me. I also told you that the responsibility for the views expressed in the address was entirely mine, and if they were not liked by the conference, I would not mind at all if the conference passed a resolution condemning them. So anxious was I to relieve your Mandal from having to assume responsibility for my views and also with the object of not getting myself entangled by too intimate an association with your conference – I suggested to you that I desired to have my address treated as a sort of an inaugural address and not as a presidential address and that the Mandal should find someone else to preside over the conference and deal with the resolutions. Nobody could have been better placed to take a decision on the 14th than your committee. The committee failed to do that, and in the meantime, cost of printing has been incurred, which, I am sure, with a little more firmness on the part of your committee, could have been saved.

I feel sure that the views expressed in my address have little to do with the decision of your committee. I have reason to believe that my presence at the Sikh Prachar Conference held at Amritsar has had a good deal to do with the decision of the committee. Nothing else can satisfactorily explain the sudden volte-face shown by the committee between the 14th and the 22nd April. I must not, however, prolong this controversy and must request you to announce immediately that the session of the conference which was to meet under my presidentship is cancelled. All the grace has by now run out, and I shall not consent to preside, even if your committee agreed to accept my address as it is, *in toto*.

I thank you for your appreciation of the pains I have taken in the preparation of the address. I certainly have profited by the labour, if no one else does. My only regret is that I was put to such hard labour at a time when my health was not equal to the strain it has caused.

Yours sincerely,
B.R. Ambedkar

This correspondence will disclose the reasons which have led to the cancellation by the Mandal of my appointment as president, and the reader will be in a position to lay the blame where it ought properly to belong. This is, I believe, the first time when the appointment of a president is cancelled by the reception committee because it does not approve of the views of the president. But whether that is so or not, this is certainly the first time in my life to have been invited to preside over a conference of caste Hindus. I am sorry that it has ended in a tragedy. But what can anyone expect from a relationship so tragic as the relationship between the reforming sect of caste Hindus and the self-respecting sect of Untouchables, where the former have no desire to alienate their orthodox fellows, and the latter have no alternative but to insist upon reform being carried out?

B.R. Ambedkar

Rajgriha, Dadar
Bombay–14
15 May 1936

# 1

## 1.1

Friends, I am really sorry for the members of the Jat-Pat Todak Mandal who have so very kindly invited me to preside over this conference. I am sure they will be asked many questions for having selected me as the president. The Mandal will be asked to explain as to why it has imported a man from Bombay to preside over a function which is held in Lahore. I believe the Mandal could easily have found someone better qualified than myself to preside on the occasion. I have criticised the Hindus. I have questioned the authority of the Mahatma whom they revere. They hate me. To them, I am a snake in their garden. The Mandal will no doubt be asked by the politically minded Hindus to explain why it has called me to fill this place of honour. It is an act of great daring. I shall not be surprised if some political Hindus regard it as an insult. This selection of mine certainly cannot please the ordinary religiously minded Hindus.

## 1.2

The Mandal may be asked to explain why it has disobeyed the shastric injunction in selecting the president. According to the Shastras, the Brahmin is appointed to be the guru for the three varnas, वर्णानाम ब्राह्मणो गुरु, is a direction of the Shastras. The Mandal, therefore, knows from whom a Hindu should take his lessons and from whom he should not. The Shastras do not permit a Hindu to accept anyone as his guru merely because he is well-versed. This is made very clear by Ramdas, a Brahmin saint from Maharashtra, who is alleged to have inspired Shivaji to establish a Hindu Raj. In his *Dasbodh*, a socio-politico-religious treatise in Marathi verse, Ramdas asks, addressing the Hindus, can we accept an *antyaja* to be our guru because he is a pandit (i.e., learned)? He gives an answer in the negative.

## 1.3

What replies to give to these questions is a matter which I must leave to the Mandal. The Mandal knows best the reasons which led it to travel to Bombay to select a president, to fix upon a man so repugnant to the Hindus and to descend so low in the scale as to select an antyaja – an Untouchable – to address an audience of the Savarnas. As for myself, you will allow me to say that I have accepted the invitation much against my will and also against the will of many of my fellow Untouchables. I know that the Hindus are sick of me. I know that I am not a *persona grata* with them. Knowing all this, I have deliberately kept myself away from them. I have no desire to inflict myself upon them. I have been giving expression to my views from my own platform. This has already caused a great deal of heartburn and irritation.

## 1.4

I have no desire to ascend the platform of the Hindus, to do within their sight what I have been doing within their hearing. If I am here, it is because of your choice and not because of my wish. Yours is a cause of social reform. That cause has always made an appeal to me, and it is because of this that I felt I ought not to refuse an opportunity of helping the cause – especially when you think that I can help it. Whether what I am going to say today will help you in any way to solve the problem you are grappling with is for you to judge. All I hope to do is to place before you my views on the problem.

# 2

## 2.1

The path of social reform, like the path to heaven (at any rate, in India), is strewn with many difficulties. Social reform in India has few friends and many critics. The critics fall into two distinct classes. One class consists of political reformers and the other of the socialists.

## 2.2

It was at one time recognised that without social efficiency, no permanent progress in the other fields of activity was possible; that, owing to mischief wrought by evil customs, Hindu society was not in a state of efficiency; and that ceaseless efforts must be made to eradicate these evils. It was due to the recognition of this fact that the birth of the National Congress was accompanied by the foundation of the Social Conference. While the Congress was concerned with defining the weak points in the political organisation of the country, the Social Conference was engaged in removing the weak points in the social organisation of Hindu society. For some time, the Congress and the Conference worked as two wings of one common activity, and they held their annual sessions in the same pandal.

## 2.3

But soon, the two wings developed into two parties, a "political reform party" and a "social reform party," between whom there raged a fierce controversy. The "political reform party" supported the National Congress, and the "social reform party" supported the Social Conference. The two bodies thus became two hostile camps. The point at issue was whether social reform should precede political reform. For a decade, the forces were evenly balanced, and the battle was fought without a victory to either side.

## 2.4

It was, however, evident that the fortunes of the Social Conference were ebbing fast. The gentlemen who presided over the sessions of the Social Conference lamented that the majority of the educated Hindus were for political advancement and indifferent to social reform; and that while the number of those who attended the Congress was very large, and the number who did not attend but who sympathised with it was even larger, the number of those who attended the Social Conference was very much smaller.

## 2.5

This indifference – this thinning of its ranks was soon followed by active hostility from the politicians. Under the leadership of the late Mr. Tilak, the courtesy with which the Congress allowed the Social Conference the use of its pandal was withdrawn, and the spirit of enmity went to such a pitch that when the Social Conference desired to erect its own pandal, a threat to burn the pandal was held out by its opponents. Thus, in the course of time, the party in favour of political reform won, and the Social Conference vanished and was forgotten.

## 2.6

The speech delivered by Mr. W.C. Bonnerjee in 1892 at Allahabad, as president of the eighth session of the Congress, sounds like a funeral oration on the death of the Social Conference and is so typical of the Congress attitude that I venture to quote from it the following extract. Mr. Bonnerjee said:

"I, for one, have no patience with those who say we shall not be fit for political reform until we reform our social system. I fail to see any connection between the two... Are we not fit (for political reform) because our widows remain unmarried and our girls are given in marriage earlier than in other countries?... because our wives and daughters do not drive about with us visiting our friends?... because we do not send our daughters to Oxford and Cambridge?"

(Cheers from the audience)

## 2.7

I have stated the case for political reform as put by Mr. Bonnerjee. There were many who were happy that the victory went to the Congress. But those who believe in the importance of social reform may ask, is an argument such as that of Mr. Bonnerjee final? Does it prove that the victory went to those who were in the right? Does it prove conclusively that social reform has no bearing on political reform? It will help us to understand the matter if I state the other side of the case. I will draw upon the treatment of the Untouchables for my facts.

## 2.8

Under the rule of the Peshwas in the Maratha country, the Untouchable was not allowed to use the public streets if a Hindu was coming along, lest he should pollute the Hindu by his shadow.

The Untouchable was required to have a black thread either on his wrist or around his neck, as a sign or a mark to prevent the Hindus from getting themselves polluted by his touch by mistake. In Poona, the capital of the Peshwa, the Untouchable was required to carry, strung from his waist, a broom to sweep away from behind himself the dust he trod on, lest a Hindu walking on the same dust should be polluted. In Poona, the Untouchable was required to carry an earthen pot hung around his neck wherever he went – for holding his spit, lest his spit falling on the earth should pollute a Hindu who might unknowingly happen to tread on it.

## 2.9

Let me take more recent facts. The tyranny practised by the Hindus upon the Balais, an Untouchable community in Central India, will serve my purpose. You will find a report of this in The *Times of India* of 4th January 1928. The correspondent of The *Times of India* reported that high-caste Hindus – viz, Kalotas, Rajputs and Brahmins, including the Patels and Patwaris of the villages of Kanaria, Bicholi-Hapsi, Bicholi-Mardana and about fifteen other villages in Indore district (of Indore State) – informed the Balais of their respective villages that if they wished to live among them, they must conform to the following rules:

1. Balais must not wear gold-lace–bordered pugrees.
2. They must not wear dhotis with coloured or fancy borders.
3. They must convey intimation of the death of any Hindu to relatives of the deceased – no matter how far away these relatives may be living.
4. In all Hindu marriages, Balais must play music before the processions and during the marriage.
5. Balai women must not wear gold or silver ornaments; they must not wear fancy gowns or jackets.
6. Balai women must attend all cases of confinement of Hindu women.
7. Balais must render services without demanding remuneration and must accept whatever a Hindu is pleased to give.
8. If the Balais do not agree to abide by these terms, they must clear out of the villages.

## 2.10

The Balais refused to comply; and the Hindu element proceeded against them. Balais were not allowed to get water from the village wells; they were not allowed to let their cattle graze. Balais were prohibited from passing through land owned by a Hindu, so that if the field of a Balai was surrounded by fields owned by Hindus, the Balai could have no access to his own field. The Hindus also let their cattle graze down the fields of Balais. The Balais submitted petitions to the Darbar against these persecutions; but as they could get no timely relief, and the oppression continued, hundreds of Balais with their wives and children were obliged to abandon their homes – in which their ancestors had lived for generations – and to migrate to adjoining states: that is, to villages in Dhar, Dewas, Bagli, Bhopal, Gwalior and other states. What happened to them in their new homes may, for the present, be left out of our consideration.

## 2.11

The incident at Kavitha in Gujarat happened only last year. The Hindus of Kavitha ordered the Untouchables not to insist upon sending their children to the common village school maintained by the government. What sufferings the Untouchables of Kavitha had to undergo, for daring to exercise a civic right against the wishes of the Hindus, is too well known to need detailed description. Another instance occurred in the village of Zanu, in the Ahmedabad district of Gujarat. In November 1935, some Untouchable women of well-to-do families started fetching water in metal pots. The Hindus looked upon the use of metal pots by Untouchables as an affront to their dignity and assaulted the Untouchable women for their impudence.

## 2.12

A most recent event is reported from the village of Chakwara in Jaipur state. It seems from the reports that have appeared in the newspapers that an Untouchable of Chakwara, who had returned from a pilgrimage, had arranged to give a dinner to his fellow Untouchables of the village, as an act of religious piety. The host desired to treat the guests to a sumptuous meal, and the items served included ghee (butter) also. But while the assembly of Untouchables was engaged in partaking of the food, the Hindus in their hundreds, armed with lathis, rushed to the scene, despoiled the food and belaboured the Untouchables who left the food and ran for their lives. And why was this murderous assault committed on defenceless Untouchables? The reason given is that the Untouchable host was impudent enough to serve ghee, and his Untouchable guests were foolish enough to taste it. Ghee is undoubtedly a luxury for the rich. But no one would think that consumption of ghee was a mark of high social status. The Hindus of Chakwara thought otherwise and, in righteous indignation, avenged themselves for the wrong done to them by the Untouchables, who insulted them by treating ghee as an item of their food – which they ought to have known could not be theirs – consistently with the dignity of the Hindus. This means that an Untouchable must not use ghee, even if he can afford to buy it, since it is an act of arrogance towards the Hindus. This happened on or about the 1st of April 1936!

## 2.13

Having stated the facts, let me now state the case for social reform. In doing this, I will follow Mr. Bonnerjee as nearly as I can, and ask the politically-minded Hindus, "Are you fit for political power even though you do not allow a large class of your own countrymen, like the Untouchables, to use public schools? Are you fit for political power even though you do not allow them the use of public wells? Are you fit for political power even though you do not allow them the use of public streets? Are you fit for political power even though you do not allow them to wear what apparel or ornaments they like? Are you fit for political power even though you do not allow them to eat any food they like?" I can ask a string of such questions. But these will suffice.

## 2.14

I wonder what would have been the reply of Mr. Bonnerjee. I am sure no sensible man will have the courage to give an affirmative answer. Every Congressman who repeats the dogma of Mill that one country is not fit to rule another country must admit that one class is not fit to rule another class. How is it then that the "social reform party" lost the battle? To understand this correctly, it is necessary to take note of the kind of social reform which the reformers were agitating for. In this connection, it is necessary to make a distinction between social reform in the sense of the reform of the Hindu family and social reform in the sense of the reorganisation and reconstruction of Hindu society. The former has a relation to widow remarriage, child marriage, etc., while the latter relates to the abolition of the caste system.

## 2.15

The Social Conference was a body which mainly concerned itself with the reform of the high caste Hindu family. It consisted mostly of enlightened high-caste Hindus who did not feel the necessity for agitating for the abolition of caste or had not the courage to agitate for it. They felt quite naturally a greater urge to remove such evils as enforced widowhood, child marriages, etc – evils which prevailed among them and which were personally felt by them. They did not stand up for the reform of Hindu society. The battle that was fought centred round the question of the reform of the family. It did not relate to social reform in the sense of the break-up of the caste system. It was never put in issue by the reformers. That is the reason why the "social reform party" lost.

## 2.16

I am aware that this argument cannot alter the fact that political reform did, in fact, gain precedence over social reform. But the argument has this much value, if not more: it explains why social reformers lost the battle. It also helps us to understand how limited was the victory which the "political reform party" obtained over the "social reform party" and to understand that the view that social reform need not precede political reform is a view which may stand only when by social reform is meant the reform of the family. That political reform cannot with impunity take precedence over social reform in the sense of the reconstruction of society is a thesis which I am sure cannot be controverted.

## 2.17

That the makers of political constitutions must take account of social forces is a fact which is recognised by no less a person than Ferdinand Lassalle, the friend and co-worker of Karl Marx. In addressing a Prussian audience in 1862, Lassalle said:

"The constitutional questions are, in the first instance, not questions of right but questions of might. The actual constitution of a country has its existence only in the actual condition of force which exists in the country: hence, political constitutions have value and permanence only when they accurately express those conditions of forces which exist in practice within a society."

## 2.18

But it is not necessary to go to Prussia. There is evidence at home. What is the significance of the Communal Award, with its allocation of political power in defined proportions to diverse classes and communities? In my view, its significance lies in this: that the political constitution must take note of social organisation. It shows that the politicians who denied that the social problem in India had any bearing on the political problem were forced to reckon with the social problem in devising the constitution. The Communal Award is, so to say, the nemesis following upon the indifference to and neglect of social reform. It is a victory for the "social reform party," which shows that, though defeated, they were in the right in insisting upon the importance of social reform. Many, I know, will not accept this finding. The view is current, and it is pleasant to believe in it that the Communal Award is unnatural and that it is the result of an unholy alliance between the minorities and the bureaucracy. I do not wish to rely on the Communal Award as a piece of evidence to support my contention, if it is said that it is not good evidence.

## 2.19

Let us turn to Ireland. What does the history of Irish Home Rule show? It is well known that in the course of the negotiations between the representatives of Ulster and Southern Ireland, Mr. Redmond, the representative of Southern Ireland, in order to bring Ulster into a Home Rule constitution common to the whole of Ireland, said to the representatives of Ulster: "Ask any political safeguards you like and you shall have them." What was the reply that Ulstermen gave? Their reply was, "Damn your safeguards, we don't want to be ruled by you on any terms."

People who blame the minorities in India ought to consider what would have happened to the political aspirations of the majority if the minorities had taken the attitude which Ulster took. Judged by the attitude of Ulster to Irish Home Rule, is it nothing that the minorities agreed to be ruled by the majority (which has not shown much sense of statesmanship), provided some safeguards were devised for them? But this is only incidental. The main question is, why did Ulster take this attitude? The only answer I can give is that there was a social problem between Ulster and Southern Ireland: the problem between Catholics and Protestants, which is essentially a problem of caste. That Home Rule in Ireland would be Rome Rule was the way in which the Ulstermen had framed their answer. But that is only another way of stating that it was the social problem of caste between the Catholics and Protestants, which prevented the solution of the political problem. This evidence again, is sure to be challenged. It will be urged that here, too, the hand of the Imperialist was at work.

## 2.20

But my resources are not exhausted. I will give evidence from the history of Rome. Here, no one can say that any evil genius was at work. Anyone who has studied the history of Rome will know that the republican constitution of Rome bore marks having a strong resemblance to the Communal Award. When the kingship in Rome was abolished, the kingly power or the Imperium was divided between the consuls and the Pontifex Maximus. In the consuls was vested the secular authority of the king, while the latter took over the religious authority of the king. This republican constitution had provided that of the two consuls, one was to be patrician and the other plebeian. The same constitution had also provided that of the priests under the Pontifex Maximus, half were to be plebeians and the other half patricians. Why is it that the republican constitution of Rome had these provisions - which, as I said, resemble so strongly the provisions of the Communal Award? The only answer one can get is that the constitution of republican Rome had to take account of the social division between the patricians and the plebeians, who formed two distinct castes. To sum up, let political reformers turn in any direction they like, they will find that in the making of a constitution, they cannot ignore the problem arising out of the prevailing social order.

## 2.21

The illustrations which I have taken in support of the proposition that social and religious problems have a bearing on political constitutions seem to be too particular. Perhaps they are. But it should not be supposed that the bearing of the one on the other is limited. On the other hand, one can say that, generally speaking, history bears out the proposition that political revolutions have always been preceded by social and religious revolutions. The religious reformation started by Luther was the precursor of the political emancipation of the European people. In England, Puritanism led to the establishment of political liberty. Puritanism founded the New World. It was Puritanism which won the War of American Independence, and Puritanism was a religious movement.

## 2.22

The same is true of the Muslim empire. Before the Arabs became a political power, they had undergone a thorough religious revolution started by the Prophet Muhammad. Even Indian history supports the same conclusion. The political revolution led by Chandragupta was preceded by the religious and social revolution of Buddha. The political revolution led by Shivaji was preceded by the religious and social reform brought about by the saints of Maharashtra. The political revolution of the Sikhs was preceded by the religious and social revolution led by Guru Nanak. It is unnecessary to add more illustrations. These will suffice to show that the emancipation of the mind and the soul is a necessary preliminary for the political expansion of the people.

# 3

## 3.1

Let me now turn to the socialists. Can the socialists ignore the problem arising out of the social order? The socialists of India, following their fellows in Europe, are seeking to apply the economic interpretation of history to the facts of India. They propound that man is an economic creature, that his activities and aspirations are bound by economic facts, that property is the only source of power. They, therefore, preach that political and social reforms are but gigantic illusions and that economic reform by equalisation of property must have precedence over every other kind of reform. One may join issue with every one of these premises – on which rests the socialists' case for economic reform as having priority over every other kind of reform. One may contend that the economic motive is not the only motive by which man is actuated. That economic power is the only kind of power; no student of human society can accept.

## 3.2

That the social status of an individual by itself often becomes a source of power and authority is made clear by the sway which the Mahatmas have held over the common man. Why do millionaires in India obey penniless sadhus and fakirs? Why do millions of paupers in India sell their trifling trinkets, which constitute their only wealth, and go to Benares and Mecca? That religion is the source of power is illustrated by the history of India, where the priest holds sway over the common man often greater than that of the magistrate, and where everything, even such things as strikes and elections, so easily takes a religious turn and can so easily be given a religious twist.

## 3.3

Take the case of the plebeians of Rome as a further illustration of the power of religion over man. It throws great light on this point. The plebeians had fought for a share in the supreme executive under the Roman Republic and had secured the appointment of a plebeian consul elected by a separate electorate constituted by the Comitia Centuriata, which was an assembly of plebeians. They wanted a consul of their own because they felt that the patrician consuls used to discriminate against the plebeians in carrying on the administration. They had apparently obtained a great gain, because under the republican constitution of Rome, one consul had the power of vetoing an act of the other consul.

## 3.4

But did they, in fact, gain anything? The answer to this question must be in the negative. The plebeians never could get a plebeian consul who could be said to be a strong man and who could act independently of the patrician consul. In the ordinary course of things, the plebeians should have got a strong plebeian consul, in view of the fact that his election was to be by a separate electorate of plebeians. The question is, why did they fail in getting a strong plebeian to officiate as their consul?

## 3.5

The answer to this question reveals the dominion which religion exercises over the minds of men. It was an accepted creed of the whole Roman populace that no official could enter upon the duties of his office unless the Oracle of Delphi declared that he was acceptable to the goddess. The priests who were in charge of the temple of the goddess of Delphi were all patricians. Whenever, therefore, the plebeians elected a consul who was known to be a strong party man and opposed to the patricians – or "communal," to use the term that is current in India – the Oracle invariably declared that he was not acceptable to the goddess. This is how the plebeians were cheated out of their rights.

## 3.6

But what is worthy of note is that the plebeians permitted themselves to be thus cheated because they too, like the patricians, held firmly the belief that the approval of the goddess was a condition precedent to the taking charge by an official of his duties and that election by the people was not enough. If the plebeians had contended that election was enough and that the approval by the goddess was not necessary, they would have derived the fullest benefit from the political right which they had obtained. But they did not. They agreed to elect another, less suitable to themselves but more suitable to the goddess – which in fact meant more amenable to the patricians. Rather than give up religion, the plebeians gave up the material gain for which they had fought so hard. Does this not show that religion can be a source of power as great as money, if not greater?

## 3.7

The fallacy of the socialists lies in supposing that, because in the present stage of European society, property as a source of power is predominant, the same is true of India, or the same was true of Europe in the past. Religion, social status and property are all sources of power and authority which one man has to control the liberty of another. One is predominant at one stage; the other is predominant at another stage. That is the only difference. If liberty is the ideal, and if liberty means the destruction of the dominion which one man holds over another, then obviously, it cannot be insisted upon that economic reform must be the one kind of reform worthy of pursuit. If the source of power and dominion is, at any given time or in any given society, social and religious, then social reform and religious reform must be accepted as the necessary sort of reform.

## 3.8

One can thus attack the doctrine of economic interpretation of history adopted by the socialists of India. But I recognise that the economic interpretation of history is not necessary for the validity of the socialist contention that equalisation of property is the only real reform and that it must precede everything else. However, what I would like to ask the socialists is this: Can you have economic reform without first bringing about a reform of the social order? The socialists of India do not seem to have considered this question. I do not wish to do them an injustice. I give below a quotation from a letter which a prominent socialist wrote a few days ago to a friend of mine, in which he said, "I do not believe that we can build up a free society in India so long as there is a trace of this ill-treatment and suppression of one class by another. Believing as I do in a socialist ideal, inevitably, I believe in perfect equality in the treatment of various classes and groups. I think that socialism offers the only true remedy for this, as well as other problems."

## 3.9

Now, the question that I would like to ask is: Is it enough for a socialist to say, "I believe in perfect equality in the treatment of the various classes?" To say that such a belief is enough is to disclose a complete lack of understanding of what is involved in socialism. If socialism is a practical programme and is not merely an ideal, distant and far off, the question for a socialist is not whether he believes in equality. The question for him is whether he minds one class illtreating and suppressing another class as a matter of system, as a matter of principle – and thus allow tyranny and oppression to continue to divide one class from another.

## 3.10

Let me analyse the factors that are involved in the realisation of socialism, in order to explain fully my point. Now, it is obvious that the economic reform contemplated by the socialists cannot come about unless there is a revolution resulting in the seizure of power. That seizure of power must be by the proletariat. The first question I ask is: Will the proletariat of India combine to bring about this revolution? What will move men to such an action? It seems to me that, other things being equal, the only thing that will move one man to take such an action is the feeling that other men with whom he is acting are actuated by feelings of equality and fraternity and – above all – of justice. Men will not join in a revolution for the equalisation of property unless they know that after the revolution is achieved, they will be treated equally and that there will be no discrimination of caste and creed.

## 3.11

The assurance of a socialist leading the revolution that he does not believe in caste, I am sure, will not suffice. The assurance must be the assurance proceeding from a much deeper foundation – namely, the mental attitude of the compatriots towards one another in their spirit of personal equality and fraternity. Can it be said that the proletariat of India, poor as it is, recognises no distinctions except that of the rich and the poor? Can it be said that the poor in India recognise no such distinctions of caste or creed, high or low? If the fact is that they do, what unity of front can be expected from such a proletariat in its action against the rich? How can there be a revolution if the proletariat cannot present a united front?

## 3.12

Suppose, for the sake of argument, that by some freak of fortune, a revolution does take place and the socialists come into power, will they not have to deal with the problems created by the particular social order prevalent in India? I can't see how a socialist state in India can function for a second without having to grapple with the problems created by the prejudices which make Indian people observe the distinctions of high and low, clean and unclean. If socialists are not to be content with the mouthing of fine phrases, if the socialists wish to make socialism a definite reality, then they must recognise that the problem of social reform is fundamental and that for them, there is no escape from it.

## 3.13

That the social order prevalent in India is a matter which a socialist must deal with; that unless he does so, he cannot achieve his revolution; and that if he does achieve it as a result of good fortune, he will have to grapple with the social order if he wishes to realise his ideal – is a proposition which, in my opinion, is incontrovertible. He will be compelled to take account of caste after the revolution, if he does not take account of it before the revolution. This is only another way of saying that, turn in any direction you like, caste is the monster that crosses your path. You cannot have political reform, you cannot have economic reform, unless you kill this monster.

# 4

## 4.1

It is a pity that caste, even today, has its defenders. The defences are many. It is defended on the ground that the caste system is but another name for division of labour; and if division of labour is a necessary feature of every civilised society, then it is argued that there is nothing wrong with the caste system. Now, the first thing that is to be urged against this view is that the caste system is not merely a division of labour. *It is also a division of labourers.* Civilised society undoubtedly needs division of labour. But in no civilised society is division of labour accompanied by this unnatural division of labourers into watertight compartments. The caste system is not merely a division of labourers – which is quite different from the division of labour; it is a hierarchy in which the divisions of labourers are graded one above the other. In no other country is the division of labour accompanied by this gradation of labourers.

## 4.2

There is also a third point of criticism against this view of the caste system. This division of labour is not spontaneous; it is not based on natural aptitudes. Social and individual efficiency requires us to develop the capacity of an individual to the point of competency to choose and to make his own career. This principle is violated in the caste system, insofar as it involves an attempt to appoint tasks to individuals in advance – selected not on the basis of trained original capacities, but on that of the social status of the parents.

## 4.3

Looked at from another point of view, this stratification of occupations, which is the result of the caste system, is positively pernicious. Industry is never static. It undergoes rapid and abrupt changes. With such changes, an individual must be free to change his occupation. Without such freedom to adjust himself to changing circumstances, it would be impossible for him to gain his livelihood. Now, the caste system will not allow Hindus to take to occupations where they are wanted, if they do not belong to them by heredity. If a Hindu is seen to starve rather than take to new occupations not assigned to his caste, the reason is to be found in the caste system. By not permitting readjustment of occupations, caste becomes a direct cause of much of the unemployment we see in the country.

## 4.4

As a form of division of labour, the caste system suffers from another serious defect. The division of labour brought about by the caste system is not a division based on choice. Individual sentiment, individual preference, has no place in it. It is based on the dogma of predestination. Considerations of social efficiency would compel us to recognise that the greatest evil in the industrial system is not so much poverty and the suffering that it involves, as the fact that so many persons have callings which make no appeal to those who are engaged in them. Such callings constantly provoke one to aversion, ill will and the desire to evade.

## 4.5

There are many occupations in India which, on account of the fact that they are regarded as degraded by the Hindus, provoke those who are engaged in them to aversion. There is a constant desire to evade and escape from such occupations, which arises solely because of the blighting effect which they produce upon those who follow them, owing to the slight and stigma cast upon them by the Hindu religion. What efficiency can there be in a system under which neither men's hearts nor their minds are in their work? As an economic organisation, caste is, therefore, a harmful institution, inasmuch as it involves the subordination of man's natural powers and inclinations to the exigencies of social rules.

# 5

## 5.1

Some have dug a biological trench in defence of the caste system. It is said that the object of caste was to preserve the purity of race and the purity of blood. Now, ethnologists are of the opinion that men of pure race exist nowhere and that there has been a mixture of all races in all parts of the world. Especially is this case with the people of India. Mr. D.R. Bhandarkar, in his paper on "Foreign Elements in the Hindu Population," has stated that "There is hardly a class or caste in India which has not a foreign strain in it. There is an admixture of alien blood not only among the warrior classes – the Rajputs and the Marathas – but also among the Brahmins who are under the happy delusion that they are free from all foreign elements." The caste system cannot be said to have grown as a means of preventing the admixture of races or as a means of maintaining purity of blood.

## 5.2

As a matter of fact, the caste system came into being long after the different races of India had commingled in blood and culture. To hold that distinctions of castes are really distinctions of race and to treat different castes as though they were so many different races is a gross perversion of facts. What racial affinity is there between the Brahmin of the Punjab and the Brahmin of Madras? What racial affinity is there between the Untouchable of Bengal and the Untouchable of Madras? What racial difference is there between the Brahmin of the Punjab and the Chamar of the Punjab? What racial difference is there between the Brahmin of Madras and the Pariah of Madras? The Brahmin of the Punjab is racially of the same stock as the Chamar of the Punjab, and the Brahmin of Madras is of the same race as the Pariah of Madras.

## 5.3

The caste system does not demarcate racial division. The caste system is a social division of people of the same race. Assuming it, however, to be a case of racial divisions, one may ask: What harm could there be if a mixture of races and of blood were permitted to take place in India by intermarriages between different castes? Men are no doubt divided from animals by so deep a distinction that science recognises men and animals as two distinct species. But even scientists who believe in the purity of races do not assert that the different races constitute different species of men. They are only varieties of one and the same species. As such, they can interbreed and produce an offspring which is capable of breeding and which is not sterile.

## 5.4

An immense lot of nonsense is talked about heredity and eugenics in defence of the caste system. Few would object to the caste system if it were in accord with the basic principle of eugenics, because few can object to the improvement of the race by judicious mating. But one fails to understand how the caste system secures judicious mating. The caste system is a negative thing. It merely prohibits persons belonging to different castes from intermarrying. It is not a positive method of selecting which two among a given caste should marry.

## 5.5

If caste is eugenic in origin, then the origin of sub-castes must also be eugenic. But can anyone seriously maintain that the origin of sub-castes is eugenic? I think it would be absurd to contend for such a proposition, and for a very obvious reason. If caste means race, then differences of sub-castes cannot mean differences of race, because sub-castes become *ex hypothesi* sub-divisions of one and the same race. Consequently, the bar against intermarrying and inter-dining between sub-castes cannot be for the purpose of maintaining purity of race or of blood. If sub-castes cannot be eugenic in origin, there cannot be any substance in the contention that caste is eugenic in origin.

## 5.6

Again, if caste is eugenic in origin, one can understand the bar against intermarriage. But what is the purpose of the interdict placed on inter-dining between castes and sub-castes alike? Inter-dining cannot infect blood and, therefore, cannot be the cause either of the improvement or of the deterioration of the race.

## 5.7

This shows that caste has no scientific origin and that those who are attempting to give it an eugenic basis are trying to support by science what is grossly unscientific. Even today, eugenics cannot become a practical possibility unless we have definite knowledge regarding the laws of heredity. Prof. Bateson in his *Mendel's Principles of Heredity* says, "There is nothing in the descent of the higher mental qualities to suggest that they follow any single system of transmission. It is likely that both they and the more marked developments of physical powers result rather from the coincidence of numerous factors than from the possession of any one genetic element." To argue that the caste system was eugenic in its conception is to attribute to the forefathers of present-day Hindus a knowledge of heredity which even modern scientists do not possess.

## 5.8

A tree should be judged by the fruit it yields. If caste is eugenic, what sort of a race of men should it have produced? Physically speaking, the Hindus are a $C_3$ people. They are a race of pygmies and dwarfs, stunted in stature and wanting in stamina. It is a nation nine-tenths of which is declared to be unfit for military service. This shows that the caste system does not embody the eugenics of modern scientists. It is a social system which embodies the arrogance and selfishness of a perverse section of the Hindus who were superior enough in social status to set it in fashion and who had the authority to force it on their inferiors.

# 6

## 6.1

Caste does not result in economic efficiency. Caste cannot improve and has not improved, race. Caste has, however, done one thing. It has completely disorganised and demoralised the Hindus.

## 6.2

The first and foremost thing that must be recognised is that Hindu society is a myth. The name Hindu is itself a foreign name. It was given by the Mahomedans to the natives for the purpose of distinguishing themselves. It does not occur in any Sanskrit work prior to the Mahomedan invasion. They did not feel the necessity of a common name, because they had no conception of their having constituted a community. Hindu society as such does not exist. It is only a collection of castes. Each caste is conscious of its existence. Its survival is the be-all and end-all of its existence. Castes do not even form a federation. A caste has no feeling that it is affiliated to other castes, except when there is a Hindu–Moslem riot. On all other occasions, each caste endeavours to segregate itself and to distinguish itself from other castes.

## 6.3

Each caste not only dines among itself and marries among itself, but each caste prescribes its own distinctive dress. What other explanation can there be of the innumerable styles of dress worn by the men and women of India, which so amuse the tourists? Indeed, the ideal Hindu must be like a rat living in his own hole, refusing to have any contact with others. There is an utter lack among the Hindus of what the sociologists call "consciousness of kind." There is no Hindu consciousness of kind. In every Hindu, the consciousness that exists is the consciousness of his caste. That is the reason why the Hindus cannot be said to form a society or a nation.

## 6.4

There are, however, many Indians whose patriotism does not permit them to admit that Indians are not a nation, that they are only an amorphous mass of people. They have insisted that underlying the apparent diversity, there is a fundamental unity which marks the life of the Hindus, inasmuch as there is a similarity of those habits and customs, beliefs and thoughts, which obtain all over the continent of India. Similarity in habits and customs, beliefs and thoughts, there is. But one cannot accept the conclusion that, therefore, the Hindus constitute a society. To do so is to misunderstand the essentials which go to make up a society. Men do not become a society by living in physical proximity, any more than a man ceases to be a member of his society by living so many miles away from other men.

## 6.5

Secondly, similarity in habits and customs, beliefs and thoughts is not enough to constitute men into society. Things may be passed physically from one to another like bricks. In the same way, habits and customs, beliefs and thoughts of one group may be taken over by another group, and there may thus appear a similarity between the two. Culture spreads by diffusion, and that is why one finds similarity between various primitive tribes in the matter of their habits and customs, beliefs and thoughts, although they do not live in proximity. But no one could say that because there was this similarity, the primitive tribes constituted one society. This is because similarity in certain things is not enough to constitute a society.

## 6.6

Men constitute a society because they have things which they possess in common. To have similar things is totally different from possessing things in common. And the only way by which men can come to possess things in common with one another is by being in communication with one another. This is merely another way of saying that society continues to exist by communication – indeed, in communication. To make it concrete, it is not enough if men act in a way which agrees with the acts of others. Parallel activity, even if similar, is not sufficient to bind men into a society.

## 6.7

This is proved by the fact that the festivals observed by the different castes amongst the Hindus are the same. Yet these parallel performances of similar festivals by the different castes have not bound them into one integral whole. For that purpose, what is necessary is for a man to share and participate in a common activity, so that the same emotions are aroused in him that animate the others. Making the individual a sharer or partner in the associated activity, so that he feels its success as his success, its failure as his failure, is the real thing that binds men and makes a society of them. The caste system prevents common activity; and by preventing common activity, it has prevented the Hindus from becoming a society with a unified life and a consciousness of its own being.

# 7

## 7.1

The Hindus often complain of the isolation and exclusiveness of a gang or a clique and blame them for anti-social spirit. But they conveniently forget that this anti-social spirit is the worst feature of their own caste system. One caste enjoys singing a hymn of hate against another caste as much as the Germans enjoyed singing their hymn of hate against the English during the last war. The literature of the Hindus is full of caste genealogies in which an attempt is made to give a noble origin to one caste and an ignoble origin to other castes. The Sahyadrikhanda is a notorious instance of this class of literature.

## 7.2

This anti-social spirit is not confined to caste alone. It has gone deeper and has poisoned the mutual relations of the sub-castes as well. In my province, the Golak Brahmins, Deorukha Brahmins, Karada Brahmins, Palshe Brahmins and Chitpavan Brahmins all claim to be subdivisions of the Brahmin caste. But the anti-social spirit that prevails between them is quite as marked and quite as virulent as the anti-social spirit that prevails between them and other non-Brahmin castes. There is nothing strange in this. An anti-social spirit is found wherever one group has "interests of its own" which shut it out from full interaction with other groups, so that its prevailing purpose is the protection of what it has got.

## 7.3

This anti-social spirit, this spirit of protecting their own interests, is as much a marked feature of the different castes in their isolation from one another as it is of nations in their isolation. The Brahmin's primary concern is to protect "his interests" against those of the non-Brahmins; and the non-Brahmins' primary concern is to protect their interests against those of the Brahmins. The Hindus, therefore, are not merely an assortment of castes, but are so many warring groups, each living for itself and for its selfish ideal.

## 7.4

There is another feature of caste which is deplorable. The ancestors of the present-day English fought on one side or the other in the Wars of the Roses and the Cromwellian War. But the descendants of those who fought on the one side do not bear any animosity – any grudge – against the descendants of those who fought on the other side. The feud is forgotten. But the present-day non-Brahmins cannot forgive the present-day Brahmins for the insult their ancestors gave to Shivaji. The present-day Kayasthas will not forgive the present-day Brahmins for the infamy cast upon their forefathers by the forefathers of the latter. To what is this difference due? Obviously, to the caste system. The existence of caste and caste consciousness has served to keep the memory of past feuds between castes green and has prevented solidarity.

# 8

## 8.1

The recent discussion about the excluded and partially excluded areas has served to draw attention to the position of what are called the aboriginal tribes in India. They number about thirteen million, if not more. Apart from the question of whether their exclusion from the new Constitution is proper or improper, the fact still remains that these aborigines have remained in their primitive, uncivilised state in a land which boasts of a civilisation thousands of years old. Not only are they not civilised, but some of them follow pursuits which have led to their being classified as criminals.

## 8.2

Thirteen million people living in the midst of civilisation are still in a savage state and are leading the life of hereditary criminals! But the Hindus have never felt ashamed of it. This is a phenomenon which, in my view, is quite unparalleled. What is the cause of this shameful state of affairs? Why has no attempt been made to civilise these aborigines and to lead them to take to a more honourable way of making a living?

## 8.3

The Hindus will probably seek to account for this savage state of the aborigines by attributing to them congenital stupidity. They will probably not admit that the aborigines have remained savages because they had made no effort to civilise them, to give them medical aid, to reform them, to make them good citizens. But supposing a Hindu wished to do what the Christian missionary is doing for these aborigines, could he have done it? I submit not. Civilising the aborigines means adopting them as your own, living in their midst and cultivating fellow-feeling – in short, loving them. How is it possible for a Hindu to do this? His whole life is one anxious effort to preserve his caste. Caste is his precious possession, which he must save at any cost. He cannot consent to lose it by establishing contact with the aborigines, the remnants of the hateful *Anaryas* of the Vedic days.

## 8.4

Not that a Hindu could not be taught the sense of duty to fallen humanity, but the trouble is that no amount of sense of duty can enable him to overcome his duty to preserve his caste. Caste is, therefore, the real explanation as to why the Hindu has let the savage remain a savage in the midst of his civilisation without blushing, or without feeling any sense of remorse or repentance. The Hindu has not realised that these aborigines are a source of potential danger. If these savages remain savages, they may not do any harm to the Hindus. But if they are reclaimed by non-Hindus and converted to their faiths, they will swell the ranks of the enemies of the Hindus. If this happens, the Hindu will have to thank himself and his caste system.

# 9

## 9.1

Not only has the Hindu made no effort for the humanitarian cause of civilising the savages, but the higher-caste Hindus have deliberately prevented the lower castes who are within the pale of Hinduism from rising to the cultural level of the higher castes. I will give two instances, one of the Sonars and the other of the Pathare Prabhus. Both are communities quite well known in Maharashtra. Like the rest of the communities desiring to raise their status, these two communities were, at one time, endeavouring to adopt some of the ways and habits of the Brahmins.

## 9.2

The Sonars were styling themselves as Daivadnya Brahmins and were wearing their dhotis with folds in them and using the word "namaskar" for salutation. Both the folded way of wearing the dhoti and the namaskar were special to the Brahmins. The Brahmins did not like this imitation and this attempt by the Sonars to pass off as Brahmins. Under the authority of the Peshwas, the Brahmins successfully put down this attempt on the part of the Sonars to adopt the ways of the Brahmins. They even got the president of the councils of the East India Company's settlement in Bombay to issue a prohibitory order against the Sonars residing in Bombay.

## 9.3

At one time, the Pathare Prabhus had widow remarriage as a custom of their caste. This custom of widow remarriage was later on looked upon as a mark of social inferiority by some members of the caste, especially because it was contrary to the custom prevalent among the Brahmins. With the object of raising the status of their community, some Pathare Prabhus sought to stop this practice of widow remarriage that was prevalent in their caste. The community was divided into two camps, one for and the other against the innovation. The Peshwas took the side of those in favour of widow remarriage and thus virtually prohibited the Pathare Prabhus from following the ways of the Brahmins.

## 9.4

The Hindus criticise the Mahomedans for having spread their religion by the use of the sword. They also ridicule Christianity on the score of the Inquisition. But really speaking, who is better and more worthy of our respect – the Mahomedans and Christians who attempted to thrust down the throats of unwilling persons what they regarded as necessary for their salvation, or the Hindu who would not spread the light, who would endeavour to keep others in darkness, who would not consent to share his intellectual and social inheritance with those who are ready and willing to make it a part of their own make-up? I have no hesitation in saying that if the Mahomedan has been cruel, the Hindu has been mean; and meanness is worse than cruelty.

# 10

## 10.1

Whether the Hindu religion was or was not a missionary religion has been a controversial issue. Some hold the view that it was never a missionary religion. Others hold that it was. That the Hindu religion was once a missionary religion must be admitted. It could not have spread over the face of India if it were not a missionary religion. That today it is not a missionary religion is also a fact which must be accepted. The question, therefore, is not whether or not the Hindu religion was a missionary religion. The real question is, why did the Hindu religion cease to be a missionary religion?

## 10.2

My answer is this: the Hindu religion ceased to be a missionary religion when the caste system grew up among the Hindus. Caste is inconsistent with conversion. Inculcation of beliefs and dogmas is not the only problem that is involved in conversion. To find a place for the convert in the social life of the community is another and a much more important problem that arises in connection with conversion. That problem is where to place the convert, in what caste? It is a problem which must baffle every Hindu wishing to make aliens convert to his religion.

## 10.3

Unlike a club, the membership of a caste is not open to all and sundry. The law of caste confines its membership to persons born in the caste. Castes are autonomous, and there is no authority anywhere to compel a caste to admit a newcomer to its social life. Hindu society, being a collection of castes, and each caste being a closed corporation, there is no place for a convert. Thus, it is caste which has prevented the Hindus from expanding and from absorbing other religious communities. So long as caste remains, Hindu religion cannot be made a missionary religion, and *shuddhi* will be both a folly and a futility.

# 11

## 11.1

The reasons which have made shuddhi impossible for Hindus are also responsible for making *sangathan* impossible. The idea underlying sangathan is to remove from the mind of the Hindu that timidity and cowardice which so painfully mark him off from the Mahomedan and the Sikh and which have led him to adopt the low ways of treachery and cunning for protecting himself. The question naturally arises: From where does the Sikh or the Mahomedan derive his strength, which makes him brave and fearless? I am sure it is not due to the relative superiority of physical strength, diet or drill. It is due to the strength arising out of the feeling that all Sikhs will come to the rescue of a Sikh when he is in danger and that all Mahomedans will rush to save a Muslim if he is attacked.

## 11.2

The Hindu can derive no such strength. He cannot feel assured that his fellows will come to his help. Being one and fated to be alone, he remains powerless, develops timidity and cowardice and, in a fight, surrenders or runs away. The Sikh as well as the Muslim stands fearless and gives battle, because he knows that though one, he will not be alone. The presence of this belief in the one helps him to hold out, and the absence of it in the other makes him give way.

## 11.3

If you pursue this matter further and ask what is it that enables the Sikh and the Mahomedan to feel so assured, and why is the Hindu filled with such despair in the matter of help and assistance, you will find that the reasons for this difference lie in the difference in their associated mode of living. The associated mode of life practised by the Sikhs and the Mahomedans produces fellow-feeling. The associated mode of life of the Hindus does not. Among

Sikhs and Muslims, there is a social cement which makes them *bhais*. Among Hindus, there is no such cement, and one Hindu does not regard another Hindu as his bhai. This explains why a Sikh says and feels that one Sikh, or one Khalsa, is equal to *sava lakh* men. This explains why one Mahomedan is equal to a crowd of Hindus. This difference is undoubtedly a difference due to caste. So long as caste remains, there will be no sangathan; and so long as there is no sangathan, the Hindu will remain weak and meek.

## 11.4

The Hindus claim to be a very tolerant people. In my opinion, this is a mistake. On many occasions, they can be intolerant, and if on some occasions they are tolerant, that is because they are too weak to oppose or too indifferent to oppose. This indifference of the Hindus has become so much a part of their nature that a Hindu will quite meekly tolerate an insult as well as a wrong. You see amongst them, to use the words of Morris, "The great treading down the little, the strong beating down the weak, cruel men fearing not, kind men daring not and wise men caring not." With the Hindu gods all-forbearing, it is not difficult to imagine the pitiable condition of the wronged and the oppressed among the Hindus. Indifferentism is the worst kind of disease that can infect people. Why is the Hindu so indifferent? In my opinion, this indifference is the result of the caste system, which has made sangathan and cooperation even for a good cause impossible.

# 12

## 12.1

The assertion by the individual of his own opinions and beliefs, his own independence and interest – over and against group standards, group authority and group interests – is the beginning of all reform. But whether the reform will continue depends upon what scope the group affords for such individual assertion. If the group is tolerant and fair-minded in dealing with such individuals, they will continue to assert and, in the end, will succeed in converting their fellows. On the other hand, if the group is intolerant and does not bother about the means it adopts to stifle such individuals, they will perish, and the reform will die out.

## 12.2

Now, a caste has an unquestioned right to excommunicate any man who is guilty of breaking the rules of the caste; and when it is realised that excommunication involves a complete cessation of social intercourse, it will be agreed that as a form of punishment there is really little to choose between excommunication and death. No wonder individual Hindus have not had the courage to assert their independence by breaking the barriers of caste.

## 12.3

It is true that man cannot get on with his fellows. But it is also true that he cannot do without them. He would like to have the society of his fellows on his terms. If he cannot get it on his terms, then he will be ready to have it on any terms, even amounting to complete surrender. This is because he cannot do without society. A caste is ever ready to take advantage of the helplessness of a man and to insist upon complete conformity to its code in letter and in spirit.

## 12.4

A caste can easily organise itself into a conspiracy to make the life of a reformer hell; and if a conspiracy is a crime, I do not understand why such a nefarious act, as an attempt to excommunicate a person for daring to act contrary to the rules of caste, should not be made an offence punishable by law. But as it is, even law gives each caste autonomy to regulate its membership and punish dissenters with excommunication. Caste, in the hands of the orthodox, has been a powerful weapon for persecuting the reformers and for killing all reform.

# 13

## 13.1

The effect of caste on the ethics of the Hindus is simply deplorable. Caste has killed public spirit. Caste has destroyed the sense of public charity. Caste has made public opinion impossible. A Hindu's public is his caste. His responsibility is only to his caste. His loyalty is restricted only to his caste. Virtue has become caste-ridden, and morality has become caste-bound. There is no sympathy for the deserving. There is no appreciation of the meritorious. There is no charity for the needy. Suffering as such calls for no response. There is charity, but it begins with caste and ends with caste. There is sympathy, but not for men of other castes.

## 13.2

Would a Hindu acknowledge and follow the leadership of a great and good man? The case of a Mahatma apart, the answer must be that he will follow a leader if he is a man of his caste. A Brahmin will follow a leader only if he is a Brahmin, a Kayastha if he is a Kayastha and so on. The capacity to appreciate merits in a man, apart from his caste, does not exist in a Hindu. There is appreciation of virtue, but only when the man is a fellow caste-man. The whole morality is as bad as tribal morality. My caste-man, right or wrong; my caste-man, good or bad. It is not a case of standing by virtue or not standing by vice. It is a case of standing by, or not standing by, the caste. Have not Hindus committed treason against their country in the interests of their castes?

# 14

## 14.1

I would not be surprised if some of you have grown weary listening to this tiresome tale of the sad effects which caste has produced. There is nothing new in it. I will therefore turn to the constructive side of the problem. What is your ideal society if you do not want caste, is a question that is bound to be asked of you. If you ask me, my ideal would be a society based on liberty, equality and fraternity. And why not?

## 14.2

What objection can there be to fraternity? I cannot imagine any. An ideal society should be mobile, should be full of channels for conveying a change taking place in one part to other parts. In an ideal society, there should be many interests consciously communicated and shared. There should be varied and free points of contact with other modes of association. In other words, there must be social endosmosis. This is fraternity, which is only another name for democracy. Democracy is not merely a form of government. It is primarily a mode of associated living, of conjoint communicated experience. It is essentially an attitude of respect and reverence towards fellow men.

## 14.3

Any objection to liberty? Few object to liberty in the sense of a right to free movement, in the sense of a right to life and limb. There is no objection to liberty in the sense of a right to property, tools and materials, as being necessary for earning a living, to keep the body in a due state of health. Why not allow a person the liberty to benefit from an effective and competent use of a person's powers? The supporters of caste who would allow liberty in the sense of a right to life, limb and property, would not readily consent to liberty in this sense, inasmuch as it involves liberty to choose one's profession.

## 14.4

But to object to this kind of liberty is to perpetuate slavery. For slavery does not merely mean a legalised form of subjection. It means a state of society in which some men are forced to accept from others the purposes which control their conduct. This condition obtains even where there is no slavery in the legal sense. It is found where, as in the caste system, some persons are compelled to carry on certain prescribed callings which are not of their choice.

## 14.5

Any objection to equality? This has obviously been the most contentious part of the slogan of the French Revolution. The objections to equality may be sound, and one may have to admit that all men are not equal. But what of that? Equality may be a fiction, but nonetheless, one must accept it as the governing principle. A man's power is dependent upon (1) physical heredity; (2) social inheritance or endowment in the form of parental care, education, accumulation of scientific knowledge, everything which enables him to be more efficient than the savage; and finally, (3) on his own efforts. In all these three respects, men are undoubtedly unequal. But the question is, shall we treat them as unequal because they are unequal? This is a question which the opponents of equality must answer.

## 14.6

From the standpoint of the individualist, it may be just to treat men unequally so far as their efforts are unequal. It may be desirable to give as much incentive as possible to the full development of everyone's powers. But what would happen if men were treated as unequally as they are unequal in the first two respects? It is obvious that those individuals also in whose favour there is birth, education, family name, business connections and inherited wealth, would be selected in the race. But selection under such circumstances would not be a selection of the able. It would be the selection of the privileged. The reason, therefore, which forces that in the third respect we should treat men unequally, demands that in the first two respects we should treat men as equally as possible.

## 14.7

On the other hand, it can be urged that if it is good for the social body to get the most out of its members, it can get the most out of them only by making them equal as far as possible at the very start of the race. That is one reason why we cannot escape equality. But there is another reason why we must accept equality. A statesman is concerned with vast numbers of people. He has neither the time nor the knowledge to draw fine distinctions and to treat each one equitably, i.e., according to need or according to capacity. However desirable or reasonable an equitable treatment of men may be, humanity is not capable of assortment and classification. The statesman, therefore, must follow some rough and ready rule, and that rough and ready rule is to treat all men alike, not because they are alike, but because classification and assortment is impossible. The doctrine of equality is glaringly fallacious, but, taking all in all, it is the only way a statesman can proceed in politics – which is a severely practical affair and which demands a severely practical test.

# 15

## 15.1

But there is a set of reformers who hold out a different ideal. They go by the name of the Arya Samajists, and their ideal of social organisation is what is called *Chaturvarnya*, or the division of society into four classes instead of the four thousand castes that we have in India. To make it more attractive and to disarm opposition, the protagonists of Chaturvarnya take great care to point out that their Chaturvarnya is based not on birth but on *guna* (worth). At the outset, I must confess that, notwithstanding the worth-basis of this Chaturvarnya, it is an ideal to which I cannot reconcile myself.

## 15.2

In the first place, if under the Chaturvarnya of the Arya Samajists, an individual is to take his place in Hindu society according to his worth, I do not understand why the Arya Samajists insist upon labelling men as Brahmin, Kshatriya, Vaishya and Shudra. A learned man would be honoured without his being labelled a Brahmin. A soldier would be respected without his being designated a Kshatriya. If European society honours its soldiers and its servants without giving them permanent labels, why should Hindu society find it difficult to do so, is a question which Arya Samajists have not cared to consider.

## 15.3

There is another objection to the continuance of these labels. All reform consists in a change in the notions, sentiments and mental attitudes of the people towards men and things. It is a common experience that certain names become associated with certain notions and sentiments which determine a person's attitude towards men and things. The names Brahmin, Kshatriya, Vaishya and Shudra are names which are associated with a definite and fixed notion in the mind of every Hindu. That notion is that of a hierarchy based on birth.

## 15.4

So long as these names continue, Hindus will continue to think of the Brahmin, Kshatriya, Vaishya and Shudra as hierarchical divisions of high and low, based on birth and to act accordingly. The Hindu must be made to unlearn all this. But how can this happen if the old labels remain and continue to recall to his mind old notions? If new notions are to be inculcated in the minds of people, it is necessary to give them new names. To continue the old names is to make the reform futile. To allow this Chaturvarnya based on worth to be designated by such stinking labels as Brahmin, Kshatriya, Vaishya, Shudra, indicative of social divisions based on birth, is a snare.

# 16

## 16.1

To me, this Chaturvarnya with its old labels is utterly repellent, and my whole being rebels against it. But I do not wish to rest my objection to Chaturvarnya on mere grounds of sentiments. There are more solid grounds on which I rely for my opposition to it. A close examination of this ideal has convinced me that as a system of social organisation, Chaturvarnya is impracticable, is harmful and has turned out to be a miserable failure. From a practical point of view, the system of Chaturvarnya raises several difficulties which its protagonists do not seem to have taken into account. The principle underlying caste is fundamentally different from the principle underlying Chaturvarnya. Not only are they fundamentally different, but they are also fundamentally opposed.

## 16.2

The former, Chaturvarnya, is based on worth. How are you going to compel people who have acquired a higher status based on birth, without reference to their worth, to vacate that status? How are you going to compel people to recognise the status due to a man, in accordance with his worth, who is occupying a lower status based on his birth? For this, you must first break up the caste system in order to be able to establish the Chaturvarnya system. How are you going to reduce the four thousand castes, based on birth, to the four varnas, based on worth? This is the first difficulty which the protagonists of Chaturvarnya must grapple with.

## 16.3

There is a second difficulty which the protagonists of Chaturvarnya must grapple with if they wish to make the establishment of Chaturvarnya a success. Chaturvarnya presupposes that you can classify people into four definite classes.

Is this possible? In this respect, the ideal of Chaturvarnya has, as you will see, a close affinity to the Platonic ideal. To Plato, men fell by nature into three classes. In some individuals, he believed, mere appetites dominated. He assigned them to the labouring and trading classes. Others revealed to him that over and above appetites, they had a courageous disposition. He classed them as defenders in war and guardians of internal peace. Others showed a capacity to grasp the universal reason underlying things. He made them the law-givers of the people.

## 16.4

The criticism to which Plato's *Republic* is subject is also the criticism which must apply to the system of Chaturvarnya, in so far as it proceeds upon the possibility of an accurate classification of men into four distinct classes. The chief criticism against Plato is that his idea of lumping individuals into a few sharply marked-off classes is a very superficial view of man and his powers. Plato had no perception of the uniqueness of every individual, of his incommensurability with others, of each individual as forming a class of his own. He had no recognition of the infinite diversity of active tendencies, and the combination of tendencies of which an individual is capable. To him, there were types of faculties or powers in the individual constitution.

## 16.5

All this is demonstrably wrong. Modern science has shown that the lumping together of individuals into a few sharply marked-off classes is a superficial view of man, not worthy of serious consideration. Consequently, the utilisation of the qualities of individuals is incompatible with their stratification by classes, since the qualities of individuals are so variable. Chaturvarnya must fail for the very reason for which Plato's Republic must fail – namely, that it is not possible to pigeon men into holes according to class. That it is impossible to accurately classify people into four definite classes is proved by the fact that the original four classes have now become four thousand castes.

## 16.6

There is a third difficulty in the way of the establishment of the system of Chaturvarnya. How are you going to maintain the system of Chaturvarnya, supposing it was established? One important requirement for the successful working of Chaturvarnya is the maintenance of the penal system, which could maintain it by its sanction. The system of Chaturvarnya must perpetually face the problem of the transgressor. Unless there is a penalty attached to the act of transgression, men will not keep to their respective classes. The whole system will break down, being contrary to human nature. Chaturvarnya cannot subsist by its own inherent goodness. It must be enforced by law.

## 16.7

That without penal sanction, the ideal of Chaturvarnya cannot be realised is proved by the story in the Ramayana of Rama killing Shambuka. Some people seem to blame Rama because he wantonly and without reason killed Shambuka. But to blame Rama for killing Shambuka is to misunderstand the whole situation. Ram Raj was a raj based on Chaturvarnya. As a king, Rama was bound to maintain Chaturvarnya. It was his duty, therefore, to kill Shambuka, the Shudra who had transgressed his class and wanted to be a Brahmin. This is the reason why Rama killed Shambuka. But this also shows that a penal sanction is necessary for the maintenance of Chaturvarnya. Not only penal sanction is necessary, but the penalty of death is necessary. That is why Rama did not inflict on Shambuka a lesser punishment. That is why the *Manusmriti* prescribes such heavy sentences as cutting off the tongue or pouring of molten lead in the ears of the Shudra who recites or hears the Veda. The supporters of Chaturvarnya must give an assurance that they could successfully classify men and that they could induce modern society in the twentieth century to re-forge the penal sanctions of the *Manusmriti.*

## 16.8

The protagonists of Chaturvarnya do not seem to have considered what is to happen to women in their system. Are they also to be divided into four classes, Brahmin, Kshatriya, Vaishya and Shudra? Or are they to be allowed to take the status of their husbands? If the status of the woman is to be the consequence of marriage, what becomes of the underlying principle of Chaturvarnya – namely, that the status of a person should be based upon the worth of that person? If they are to be classified according to their worth, is their classification to be nominal or real?

## 16.9

If it is to be nominal, then it is useless; and then, the protagonists of Chaturvarnya must admit that their system does not apply to women. If it is real, are the protagonists of Chaturvarnya prepared to follow the logical consequences of applying it to women? They must be prepared to have women priests and women soldiers. Hindu society has grown accustomed to women teachers and women barristers. It may grow accustomed to women brewers and women butchers. But he would be a bold person who would say that it will allow women priests and women soldiers. But that will be the logical outcome of applying Chaturvarnya to women. Given these difficulties, I think no one except a congenital idiot could hope for and believe in a successful regeneration of Chaturvarnya.

# 17

## 17.1

Assuming that Chaturvarnya is practicable, I contend that it is the most vicious system. That the Brahmins should cultivate knowledge, that the Kshatriya should bear arms, that the Vaishya should trade and that the Shudra should serve sounds as though it was a system of division of labour. Whether the theory was intended to state that the Shudra need not, or whether it was intended to lay down that he must not, is an interesting question. The defenders of Chaturvarnya give it the first meaning. They say, why need the Shudra trouble to acquire wealth when the three higher varnas are there to support him? Why need the Shudra bother to take to education, when there is the Brahmin to whom he can go when the occasion for reading or writing arises? Why need the Shudra worry to arm himself when there is the Kshatriya to protect him? The theory of Chaturvarnya, understood in this sense, may be said to look upon the Shudra as the ward and the three higher varnas as his guardians. Thus interpreted, it is a simple, elevating and alluring theory.

## 17.2

Assuming this to be the correct view of the underlying conception of Chaturvarnya, it seems to me that the system is neither foolproof nor knave-proof. What is to happen if the Brahmins, Vaishyas and Kshatriyas fail to pursue knowledge, to engage in economic enterprise and to be efficient soldiers, which are their respective functions? Contrary-wise, suppose that they discharge their functions, but flout their duty to the Shudra or to one another; what is to happen to the Shudra if the three classes refuse to support him on fair terms, or combine to keep him down? Who is to safeguard the interests of the Shudra – or for that matter, those of the Vaishya and Kshatriya – when the person who is trying to take advantage of his ignorance is the Brahmin? Who is to defend the liberty of the Shudra – and for that matter, of the Brahmin and the Vaishya – when the person who is robbing him of it is the Kshatriya?

## 17.3

Interdependence of one class on another class is inevitable. Even dependence of one class upon another may sometimes become allowable. But why make one person depend upon another in the matter of his vital needs? Education, everyone must have. Means of defence, everyone must have.

These are the paramount requirements of every man for his self-preservation. How can the fact that his neighbour is educated and armed help a man who is uneducated and disarmed? The whole theory is absurd. These are the questions which the defenders of Chaturvarnya do not seem to be troubled about. But they are very pertinent questions. Assuming that, in their conception of Chaturvarnya, the relationship between the different classes is that of ward and guardian and that this is the real conception underlying Chaturvarnya, it must be admitted that it makes no provision to safeguard the interests of the ward from the misdeeds of the guardian.

## 17.4

Whether or not the relationship of guardian and ward was the real underlying conception on which Chaturvarnya was based, there is no doubt that in practice, the relation was that of master and servants. The three classes, Brahmins, Kshatriyas and Vaishyas, although not very happy in their mutual relationship, managed to work by compromise. The Brahmin flattered the Kshatriya, and both let the Vaishya live in order to be able to live upon him. But the three agreed to beat down the Shudra. He was not allowed to acquire wealth, lest he should be independent of the three varnas. He was prohibited from acquiring knowledge, lest he should keep a steady vigil regarding his interests. He was prohibited from bearing arms, lest he should have the means to rebel against their authority. That this is how the Shudras were treated by the *Tryavarnikas* is evidenced by the laws of Manu. There is no code of laws more infamous regarding social rights than the laws of Manu. Any instance from anywhere of social injustice must pale before it.

## 17.5

Why have the masses of people tolerated the social evils to which they have been subjected? There have been social revolutions in other countries of the world. Why have there not been social revolutions in India, is a question which has incessantly troubled me. There is only one answer which I can give, and it is that the lower classes of Hindus have been completely disabled from direct action on account of this wretched caste system. They could not bear arms, and without arms, they could not rebel. They were all ploughmen – or rather, condemned to be ploughmen – and they never were allowed to convert their ploughshares into swords. They had no bayonets, and therefore, everyone who chose could and did sit upon them. On account of the caste system, they could receive no education. They could not think out or know the way to their salvation. They were condemned to be lowly; and not knowing the way of escape and not having the means of escape, they became reconciled to eternal servitude, which they accepted as their inescapable fate.

## 17.6

It is true that even in Europe, the strong have not shrunk from the exploitation – nay, the spoliation – of the weak. But in Europe, the strong have never contrived to make the weak helpless against exploitation so shamelessly as was the case in India among the Hindus. Social war has been raging between the strong and the weak far more violently in Europe than it has ever been in India. Yet, the weak in Europe has had in his freedom of military service, his physical weapon; in suffering, his political weapon; and in education, his moral weapon. These three weapons for emancipation were never withheld by the strong from the weak in Europe. All these weapons were, however, denied to the masses in India by the caste system.

## 17.7

There cannot be a more degrading system of social organisation than the caste system. It is the system which deadens, paralyses and cripples the people from helpful activity. This is no exaggeration. History bears ample evidence. There is only one period in Indian history which is a period of freedom, greatness and glory. That is the period of the Maurya Empire. At all other times, the country suffered from defeat and darkness. But the Maurya period was a period when the caste system was completely annihilated – when the Shudras, who constituted the mass of the people, came into their own and became the rulers of the country. The period of defeat and darkness is the period when the caste system flourished, to the damnation of the greater part of the people of the country.

# 18

## 18.1

Chaturvarnya is not new. It is as old as the Vedas. That is one of the reasons why we are asked by the Arya Samajists to consider their claims. Judging from the past, as a system of social organisation, it has been tried, and it has failed. How many times have the Brahmins annihilated the seed of the Kshatriyas! How many times have the Kshatriyas annihilated the Brahmins! The Mahabharata and the Puranas are full of incidents of the strife between the Brahmins and the Kshatriyas. They even quarrelled over such petty questions as to who should salute first, as to who should give way first, the Brahmins or the Kshatriyas, when the two met in the street.

## 18.2

Not only was the Brahmin an eyesore to the Kshatriya and the Kshatriya an eyesore to the Brahmin, but it seems that the Kshatriyas had become tyrannical, and the masses, disarmed as they were under the system of Chaturvarnya, were praying to the almighty for relief from their tyranny. The Bhagwat tells us very definitely that Krishna had taken an avatar for one sacred purpose: and that was, to annihilate the Kshatriyas. With these instances of rivalry and enmity between the different varnas before us, I do not understand how anyone can hold out Chaturvarnya as an ideal to be aimed at, or as a pattern on which Hindu society should be remodelled.

# 19

## 19.1

I have dealt with those who are without you and whose hostility to your ideal is quite open. There appear to be others who are neither without you nor with you. I was hesitating whether I should deal with their point of view. But on further consideration, I have come to the conclusion that I must and that for two reasons. Firstly, their attitude to the problem of caste is not merely an attitude of neutrality, but is an attitude of armed neutrality. Secondly, they probably represent a considerable body of people. Of these, there is one set which finds nothing peculiar or odious in the caste system of the Hindus. Such Hindus cite the case of Muslims, Sikhs and Christians and find comfort in the fact that they too have castes amongst them.

## 19.2

In considering this question, you must at the outset bear in mind that nowhere is human society one single whole. It is always plural. In the world of action, the individual is one limit and society the other. Between them lie all sorts of associative arrangements of lesser and larger scope – families, friendships, cooperative associations, business combines, political parties, bands of thieves and robbers. These small groups are usually firmly welded together and are often as exclusive as castes. They have a narrow and intensive code, which is often anti-social. This is true of every society, in Europe as well as in Asia. The question to be asked in determining whether a given society is an ideal society is not whether there are groups in it, because groups exist in all societies.

## 19.3

The questions to be asked in determining what is an ideal society are: How numerous and varied are the interests which are consciously shared by the groups? How full and free is the interplay with other forms of associations? Are the forces that separate groups and classes more numerous than the forces that unite them? What social significance is attached to this group life? Is its exclusiveness a matter of custom and convenience, or is it a matter of religion? It is in the light of these questions that one must decide whether caste among non-Hindus is the same as caste among Hindus.

## 19.4

If we apply these considerations to castes among Mahomedans, Sikhs and Christians on the one hand and to castes among Hindus on the other, you will find that caste among non-Hindus is fundamentally different from caste among Hindus. First, the ties which consciously make the Hindus hold together are non-existent, while among non-Hindus, there are many that hold them together. The strength of a society depends upon the presence of points of contact, possibilities of interaction between different groups which exist in it. These are what Carlyle calls "organic filaments" – i.e., the elastic threads which help to bring the disintegrating elements together and to reunite them. There is no integrating force among the Hindus to counteract the disintegration caused by caste. While among the non-Hindus, there are plenty of these "organic filaments" which bind them together.

## 19.5

Again, it must be borne in mind that although there are castes among non-Hindus, as there are among Hindus, caste has not the same social significance for non-Hindus as it has for Hindus. Ask a Mahomedan or a Sikh who he is. He tells you that he is a Mahomedan or a Sikh, as the case may be. He does not tell you his caste, although he has one, and you are satisfied with his answer. When he tells you that he is a Muslim, you do not proceed to ask him whether he is a Shia or a Sunni; Sheikh or Saiyad; Khatik or Pinjari. When he tells you he is a Sikh, you do not ask him whether he is Jat or Roda; Mazbi or Ramdasi. But you are not satisfied if a person tells you that he is a Hindu. You feel bound to inquire into his caste. Why? Because so essential is caste in the case of a Hindu that, without knowing it, you do not feel sure what sort of a being he is.

## 19.6

That caste has not the same social significance among non-Hindus as it has among Hindus is clear if you take into consideration the consequences which follow breach of caste. There may be castes among Sikhs and Mahomedans, but the Sikhs and the Mahomedans will not outcast a Sikh or a Mahomedan if he broke his caste. Indeed, the very idea of excommunication is foreign to the Sikhs and the Mahomedans. But with the Hindus, the case is entirely different. A Hindu is sure to be an outcast if he breaks caste. This shows the difference in the social significance of caste to Hindus and non-Hindus. This is the second point of difference.

## 19.7

But there is also a third and a more important one. Caste among the non-Hindus has no religious consecration; but among the Hindus, most decidedly it has. Among the non-Hindus, caste is only a practice, not a sacred institution. They did not originate it. With them, it is only a survival mechanism. They do not regard caste as a religious dogma. Religion compels the Hindus to treat isolation and segregation of castes as a virtue. Religion does not compel the non-Hindus to take the same attitude towards caste. If Hindus wish to break caste, their religion will come in their way. But it will not be so in the case of non-Hindus. It is, therefore, a dangerous delusion to take comfort in the mere existence of caste among non-Hindus, without caring to know what place caste occupies in their life and whether there are other "organic filaments" which subordinate the feeling of caste to the feeling of community. The sooner the Hindus are cured of this delusion, the better.

## 19.8

The other set denies that caste presents any problem at all for the Hindus to consider. Such Hindus seek comfort in the view that the Hindus have survived and take this as proof of their fitness to survive. This point of view is well expressed by

Prof. S. Radhakrishnan in his *Hindu View of Life*. Referring to Hinduism, he says: "The civilisation itself has not been a short-lived one. Its historic records date back to over four thousand years, and even then it had reached a stage of civilisation which has continued its unbroken, though at times slow and static, course until the present day. It has stood the stress and strain of more than four or five millennia of spiritual thought and experience. Though people of different races and cultures have been pouring into India from the dawn of history, Hinduism has been able to maintain its supremacy, and even the proselytising creeds backed by political power have not been able to coerce the large majority of Hindus to their views. The Hindu culture possesses some vitality which seems to be denied to some other more forceful currents. It is no more necessary to dissect Hinduism than to open a tree to see whether the sap still runs." The name of Prof Radhakrishnan is big enough to invest with profundity whatever he says and impress the minds of his readers. But I must not hesitate to speak my mind. For I fear that his statement may become the basis of a vicious argument that the fact of survival is proof of fitness to survive.

## 19.9

It seems to me that the question is not whether a community lives or dies; the question is on what plane does it live. There are different modes of survival. But not all are equally honourable. For an individual as well as for a society, there is a gulf between merely living and living worthily. To fight in a battle and to live in glory is one mode. To beat a retreat, to surrender and to live the life of a captive is also a mode of survival. It is useless for a Hindu to take comfort in the fact that he and his people have survived. What he must consider is, what is the quality of their survival. If he does that, I am sure he will cease to take pride in the mere fact of survival. A Hindu's life has been a life of continuous defeat, and what appears to him to be life everlasting is not living everlastingly, but is really a life which is perishing everlastingly. It is a mode of survival of which every right-minded Hindu who is not afraid to own up to the truth will feel ashamed.

# 20

## 20.1

There is no doubt, in my opinion, that unless you change your social order, you can achieve little by way of progress. You cannot mobilise the community either for defence or for offence. You cannot build anything on the foundations of caste. You cannot build up a nation, you cannot build up a morality. Anything that you will build on the foundations of caste will crack, and will never be whole.

## 20.2

The only question that remains to be considered is – How to bring about the reform of the Hindu social order? How to abolish caste? This is a question of supreme importance. There is a view that in the reform of caste, the first step to take is to abolish sub castes. This view is based upon the supposition that there is a greater similarity in manners and status between sub-castes than there is between castes. I think this is an erroneous supposition. The Brahmins of Northern and Central India are socially of a lower grade, as compared with the Brahmins of the Deccan and Southern India. The former are only cooks and water-carriers, while the latter occupy a high social position. On the other hand, in Northern India, the Vaishyas and Kayasthas are intellectually and socially on a par with the Brahmins of the Deccan and Southern India.

## 20.3

Again, in the matter of food, there is no similarity between the Brahmins of the Deccan and Southern India, who are vegetarians, and the Brahmins of Kashmir and Bengal, who are non-vegetarians.

On the other hand, the Brahmins of the Deccan and Southern India have more in common, so far as food is concerned, with such non-Brahmins as the Gujaratis, Marwaris, Banias and Jains.

## 20.4

There is no doubt that from the standpoint of making the transition from one caste to another easy, the fusion of the Kayasthas of Northern India and the other non-Brahmins of Southern India with the non-Brahmins of the Deccan and the Dravidian country is more practicable than the fusion of the Brahmins of the south with the Brahmins of the north. But assuming that the fusion of sub-castes is possible, what guarantee is there that the abolition of sub-castes will necessarily lead to the abolition of castes? On the contrary, it may happen that the process may stop with the abolition of sub-castes. In that case, the abolition of sub-castes will only help to strengthen the castes and make them more powerful and, therefore, more mischievous. This remedy is, therefore, neither practicable nor effective and may easily prove to be a wrong remedy.

## 20.5

Another plan of action for the abolition of caste is to begin with inter-caste dinners. This also, in my opinion, is an inadequate remedy. There are many castes which allow inter-dining. But it is a common experience that inter-dining has not succeeded in killing the spirit of caste and the consciousness of caste. I am convinced that the real remedy is intermarriage. Fusion of blood can alone create the feeling of being kith and kin, and unless this feeling of kinship, of being kindred, becomes paramount, the separatist feeling – the feeling of being aliens – created by caste will not vanish. Among the Hindus, intermarriage must necessarily be a factor of greater force in social life than it need be in the life of the non-Hindus. Where society is already well knit by other ties, marriage is an ordinary incident of life. But where society is cut asunder, marriage as a binding force becomes a matter of urgent necessity. The real remedy for breaking caste is intermarriage. Nothing else will serve as the solvent of caste.

## 20.6

Your Jat-Pat Todak Mandal has adopted this line of attack. It is a direct and frontal attack, and I congratulate you upon a correct diagnosis and more upon your having shown the courage to tell the Hindus what is really wrong with them. Political tyranny is nothing compared to social tyranny, and a reformer who defies society is a much more courageous man than a politician who defies the government. You are right in holding that caste will cease to be an operative force only when inter-dining and intermarriage have become matters of common course. You have located the source of the disease.

## 20.7

But is your prescription the right prescription for the disease? Ask yourselves this question: Why is it that a large majority of Hindus do not inter-dine and do not intermarry? Why is it that your cause is not popular?

## 20.8

There can be only one answer to this question, and it is that inter-dining and intermarriage are repugnant to the beliefs and dogmas which the Hindus regard as sacred. Caste is not a physical object like a wall of bricks or a line of barbed wire which prevents the Hindus from commingling and which has, therefore, to be pulled down. Caste is a notion; it is a state of mind. The destruction of caste does not, therefore, mean the destruction of a physical barrier. It means a notional change.

## 20.9

Caste may be bad. Caste may lead to conduct so gross as to be called man's inhumanity to man. All the same, it must be recognised that the Hindus observe caste not because they are inhuman or wrong-headed. They observe caste because they are deeply religious. People are not wrong in observing caste. In my view, what is wrong is their religion, which has inculcated this notion of caste. If this is correct, then obviously the enemy you must grapple with is not the people who observe caste, but the Shastras which teach them this religion of caste. Criticising and ridiculing people for not inter-dining or intermarrying or occasionally holding inter-caste dinners and celebrating inter-caste marriages, is a futile method of achieving the desired end. The real remedy is to destroy the belief in the sanctity of the Shastras.

## 20.10

How do you expect to succeed if you allow the Shastras to continue to mould the beliefs and opinions of the people? Not to question the authority of the Shastras – to permit the people to believe in their sanctity and their sanctions and then to blame the people and to criticise them for their acts as being irrational and inhuman – is an incongruous way of carrying on social reform. Reformers working for the removal of untouchability, including Mahatma Gandhi, do not seem to realise that the acts of the people are merely the results of their beliefs inculcated in their minds by the Shastras and that people will not change their conduct until they cease to believe in the sanctity of the Shastras on which their conduct is founded.

## 20.11

No wonder that such efforts have not produced any results. You also seem to be erring in the same way as the reformers working in the cause of removing untouchability. To agitate for and to organise inter-caste dinners and inter-caste marriages is like forced feeding brought about by artificial means. Make every man and woman free from the thralldom of the Shastras, cleanse their minds of the pernicious notions founded on the Shastras, and he or she will inter-dine and intermarry, without your telling him or her to do so.

## 20.12

It is no use seeking refuge in quibbles. It is no use telling people that the Shastras do not say what they are believed to say, if they are grammatically read or logically interpreted. What matters is how the shastras have been understood by the people. You must take the stand that Buddha took. You must take the stand that Guru Nanak took. You must not only discard the Shastras, you must deny their authority, as did Buddha and Nanak. You must have the courage to tell the Hindus that what is wrong with them is their religion – the religion which has produced in them this notion of the sacredness of caste. Will you show that courage?

# 21

## 21.1

What are your chances of success? Social reforms fall into different species. There is a species of reform which does not relate to the religious notions of a people, but is purely secular in character. There is also a species of reform which relates to the religious notions of a people. Of such a species of reform, there are two varieties. In one, the reform accords with the principles of the religion and merely invites people who have departed from it to revert to them and to follow them.

## 21.2

The second is a reform which not only touches the religious principles but is diametrically opposed to those principles and invites people to depart from and to discard their authority and to act contrary to those principles. Caste is the natural outcome of certain religious beliefs which have the sanction of the Shastras, which are believed to contain the command of divinely inspired sages who were endowed with a supernatural wisdom and whose commands, therefore, cannot be disobeyed without committing a sin.

## 21.3

The destruction of caste is a reform which falls under the third category. To ask people to give up caste is to ask them to go contrary to their fundamental religious notions. It is obvious that the first and second species of reform are easy. But the third is a stupendous task, well-nigh impossible. The Hindus hold to the sacredness of the social order. Caste has a divine basis. You must therefore destroy the sacredness and divinity with which caste has become invested. In the last analysis, this means you must destroy the authority of the Shastras and the Vedas.

## 21.4

I have emphasised this question of the ways and means of destroying caste, because I think that knowing the proper ways and means is more important than knowing the ideal. If you do not know the real ways and means, all your shots are sure to be misfired. If my analysis is correct, then your task is Herculean. You alone can say whether you are capable of achieving it.

## 21.5

Speaking for myself, I see the task to be well-nigh impossible. Perhaps, you would like to know why I think so. Out of the many reasons which have led me to take this view, I will mention some which I regard as most important. One of these reasons is the attitude of hostility which the Brahmins have shown towards this question. The Brahmins form the vanguard of the movement for political reform and, in some cases, also of economic reform. But they are not to be found even as camp-followers in the army raised to break down the barricades of caste. Is there any hope of the Brahmins ever taking up a lead in the future in this matter? I say no.

## 21.6

You may ask why. You may argue that there is no reason why Brahmins should continue to shun social reform. You may argue that the Brahmins know that the bane of Hindu society is caste, and as an enlightened class, they could not be expected to be indifferent to its consequences. You may argue that there are secular Brahmins and priestly Brahmins, and if the latter do not take up the cudgels on behalf of those who want to break caste, the former will.

## 21.7

All this, of course, sounds very plausible. But in all this, it is forgotten that the break-up of the caste system is bound to adversely affect the Brahmin caste. Having regard to this, is it reasonable to expect that the Brahmins will ever consent to lead a movement, the ultimate result of which is to destroy the power and prestige of the Brahmin caste? Is it reasonable to expect the secular Brahmins to take part in a movement directed against the priestly Brahmins? In my judgement, it is useless to make a distinction between the secular Brahmins and priestly Brahmins. Both are kith and kin. They are two arms of the same body, and one is bound to fight for the existence of the other.

## 21.8

In this connection, I am reminded of some very pregnant remarks made by Prof. Dicey in his *English Constitution*. Speaking of the actual limitation on the legislative supremacy of parliament, Dicey says: "The actual exercise of authority by any sovereign whatever, and notably by parliament, is bounded or controlled by two limitations. Of these the one is an external; the other is an internal limitation. The external limit to the real power of a sovereign consists in the possibility or certainty that his subjects, or a large number of them, will disobey or resist his laws... The internal limit to the exercise of sovereignty arises from the nature of the sovereign power itself. Even a despot exercises his powers in accordance with his character, which is itself moulded by the circumstances under which he lives, including under that head the moral feelings of the time and the society to which he belongs. The Sultan could not, if he would, change the religion of the Mahommedan world, but even if he could do so, it is in the very highest degree improbable that the head of Mahommedanism should wish to overthrow the religion of Mahomet; the internal check on the exercise of the Sultan's power is at least as strong as the external limitation. People sometimes ask the idle question, Why does the Pope not introduce this or that reform? The true answer is that a revolutionist is not the kind of man who becomes a Pope, and that the man who becomes a Pope has no wish to be a revolutionist."

## 21.9

I think, these remarks apply equally to the Brahmins of India, and one can say with equal truth that if a man who becomes a Pope has no wish to become a revolutionary, a man who is born a Brahmin has much less desire to become a revolutionary. Indeed, to expect a Brahmin to be a revolutionary in matters of social reform is as idle as to expect the British Parliament, as was said by Leslie Stephen, to pass an Act requiring all blue-eyed babies to be murdered.

## 21.10

Some of you will say that it is a matter of small concern whether the Brahmins come forward to lead the movement against caste or whether they do not. To take this view is, in my judgement, to ignore the part played by the intellectual class in the community. Whether you accept the theory of the great man as the maker of history or whether you do not, this much you will have to concede: that in every country, the intellectual class is the most influential class, if not the governing class. The intellectual class is the class which can foresee, it is the class which can advise and give the lead. In no country does the mass of the people live the life of intelligent thought and action. It is largely imitative and follows the intellectual class.

## 21.11

There is no exaggeration in saying that the entire destiny of a country depends upon its intellectual class. If the intellectual class is honest, independent and disinterested, it can be trusted to take the initiative and give a proper lead when a crisis arises. It is true that intellect by itself is no virtue. It is only a means, and the use of means depends upon the ends which an intellectual person pursues. An intellectual man can be a good man, but he can easily be a rogue. Similarly, an intellectual class may be a band of high-souled persons, ready to help, ready to emancipate erring humanity – or it may easily be a gang of crooks, or a body of advocates for a narrow clique from which it draws its support.

## 21.12

You may think it a pity that the intellectual class in India is simply another name for the Brahmin caste. You may regret that the two are one; that the existence of the intellectual class should be bound up with one single caste; that this intellectual class should share the interest and the aspirations of that Brahmin caste, which has regarded itself as the custodian of the interest of that caste rather than of the interests of the country. All this may be very regrettable. But the fact remains that the Brahmins form the intellectual class of the Hindus. It is not only an intellectual class, but it is a class which is held in great reverence by the rest of the Hindus.

## 21.13

The Hindus are taught that the Brahmins are *Bhu-devas* (gods on earth). The Hindus are taught that Brahmins alone can be their teachers. Manu says: "If it be asked how it should be with respect to points of the Dharma which have not been specially mentioned, the answer is, that which Brahmins who are *shishthas* propound shall doubtless have legal force."

अनाम्नातेषु धर्मेषु कथं स्यादिति चेद्भवेत्।
यं शिष्टा ब्राह्मणा ब्रूयुः स धर्मः स्यादशङ्कितः॥

## 21.14

When such an intellectual class, which holds the rest of the community in its grip, is opposed to the reform of caste, the chances of success in a movement for the break-up of the caste system appear to me very, very remote.

## 21.15

The second reason why I say the task is impossible will be clear if you will bear in mind that the caste system has two aspects. In one of its aspects, it divides men into separate communities. In its second aspect, it places these communities in a graded order, one above the other in social status. Each caste takes its pride and its consolation in the fact that, in the scale of castes, it is above some other caste. As an outward mark of this gradation, there is also a gradation of social and religious rights, technically spoken of as *ashtadhikaras* and *sanskaras*. The higher the grade of a caste, the greater the number of these rights; and the lower the grade, the lesser their number.

## 21.16

Now, this gradation, this scaling of castes, makes it impossible to organise a common front against the caste system. If a caste claims the right to inter-dine and intermarry with another caste placed above it, it is frozen the instant it is told by mischief-mongers – and there are many Brahmins amongst such mischief-mongers – that it will have to concede inter-dining and intermarriage with castes below it! All are slaves of the caste system. But all the slaves are not equal in status.

## 21.17

To excite the proletariat to bring about an economic revolution, Karl Marx told them: "You have nothing to lose except your chains." But the artful way in which the social and religious rights are distributed among the different castes, whereby some have more and some have less, makes the slogan of Karl Marx quite useless to excite the Hindus against the caste system. Castes form a graded system of sovereignties, high and low, which are jealous of their status and which know that if a general dissolution came, some of them stand to lose more of their prestige and power than others do. You cannot, therefore, have a general mobilisation of the Hindus (to use a military expression) for an attack on the caste system.

# 22

## 22.1

Can you appeal to reason and ask the Hindus to discard caste as being contrary to reason? That raises the question: Is a Hindu free to follow his reason? Manu has laid down three sanctions to which every Hindu must conform in the matter of his behaviour:

वेदः स्मृतिः सदाचारः स्वस्य च प्रियमात्मनः।

## 22.2

Here, there is no place for reason to play its part. A Hindu must follow either Veda, Smriti or *sadachar*. He cannot follow anything else.

## 22.3

In the first place, how are the texts of the Vedas and Smritis to be interpreted whenever any doubt arises regarding their meaning? On this important question, the view of Manu is quite definite. He says:

योऽवमन्येत ते मूले हेतुशास्त्राश्रयाद्द्विजः।
स साधुभिर्बहिष्कार्यो नास्तिको वेदनिन्दकः॥

## 22.4

According to this rule, rationalism as a canon of interpreting the Vedas and Smritis is absolutely condemned. It is regarded to be as wicked as atheism, and the punishment provided for it is excommunication. Thus, where a matter is covered by the Veda or the Smriti, a Hindu cannot resort to rational thinking.

## 22.5

Even when there is a conflict between the Vedas and Smritis on matters on which they have given a positive injunction, the solution is not left to reason. When there is a conflict between two Shrutis, both are to be regarded as of equal authority. Either of them may be followed. No attempt is to be made to find out which of the two accords with reason. This is made clear by Manu:

श्रुतिद्वैधं तु यत्र स्यात्तत्र धर्मावुभौ स्मृतौ।
उभावपि हि तौ धर्मौ सम्यगुक्तौ मनीषिभिः।।

## 22.6

"When there is a conflict between Shruti and Smriti, Shruti must prevail." But here, too, no attempt must be made to find out which of the two accords with reason. This is laid down by Manu in the following shloka:

या वेदबाह्याः स्मृतयो याश्च काश्च कुदृष्टयः।
सर्वास्ता निष्फलाः प्रेत्य तमोनिष्ठा हि ताः स्मृताः।।

## 22.7

Again, when there is a conflict between two Smritis, the *Manusmriti* must prevail, but no attempt is to be made to find out which of the two accords with reason. This is the ruling given by Brihaspati:

वेदार्थत्वोपनिबंधूत्बात प्रामाण्यं हि मनोः स्त्रितं।
मन्वर्थविपरीता तु या स्मृतिः सा न शस्यते।।

## 22.8

It is, therefore, clear that in any matter on which the Shrutis and Smritis have given a positive direction, a Hindu is not free to use his reasoning faculty. The same rule is laid down in the Mahabharata:

पुराणं मानवो धर्मः सांगो वेदश्चिकित्सितं।
आज्ञासिद्धानि चत्वारि न हन्तव्यानि हेतुभिः।।

## 22.9

He must abide by their directions. Caste and varna are matters which are dealt with by the Vedas and the Smritis, and consequently, appeal to reason can have no effect on a Hindu.

## 22.10

So far as caste and varna are concerned, not only do the Shastras not permit the Hindu to use his reason in the decision of the question, but they have taken care to see that no occasion is left to examine in a rational way the foundations of his belief in caste and varna. It must be a source of silent amusement to many a non-Hindu to find hundreds and thousands of Hindus breaking caste on certain occasions, such as railway journeys and foreign travel, and yet endeavouring to maintain caste for the rest of their lives!

## 22.11

The explanation of this phenomenon discloses another fetter on the reasoning faculties of the Hindus. Man's life is generally habitual and unreflective. Reflective thought – in the sense of active, persistent and careful consideration of any belief or supposed form of knowledge, in the light of the grounds that support it and the further conclusions to which it tends – is quite rare, and arises only in a situation which presents a dilemma or a crisis. Railway journeys and foreign travels are really occasions of crisis in the life of a Hindu, and it is natural to expect a Hindu to ask himself why he should maintain caste at all, if he cannot maintain it at all times. But he does not. He breaks caste at one step and proceeds to observe it at the next, without raising any question.

## 22.12

The reason for this astonishing conduct is to be found in the rule of the Shastras, which directs him to maintain caste as far as possible and to undergo *prayaschitta* when he cannot. By this theory of prayaschitta, the Shastras, by following a spirit of compromise, have given caste a perpetual lease on life and have smothered the reflective thought which would have otherwise led to the destruction of the notion of caste.

## 22.13

There have been many who have worked for the cause of the abolition of caste and untouchability. Of those who can be mentioned, Ramanuja, Kabir and others stand out prominently. Can you appeal to the acts of these reformers and exhort the Hindus to follow them?

## 22.14

It is true that Manu has included (sadachar) as one of the sanctions along with shruti and smriti. Indeed, sadachar has been given a higher place than Shastras:

यद्यदाचर्यते येन धर्म्यं वा ऽधर्म्यमेव वा।
देशस्याचरणं नित्यं चरित्रं तद्धिकीर्तितम्॥

## 22.15

According to this, sadachar, whether it is in accordance with Shastras or contrary to Shastras, must be followed. But what is the meaning of sadachar? If anyone were to suppose that sadachar means right or good acts – i.e., acts of good and righteous men – he would find himself greatly mistaken. Sadachar does not mean good acts or acts of good men. It means ancient custom, good or bad. The following verse makes this clear:

यस्मिन देशे य आचारः पारंपर्यक्रमागत।
वर्णानां किल सर्वषां स सदाचार उच्यते॥

## 22.16

As though to warn people against the view that sadachar means good acts or acts of good men, and fearing that people might understand it that way and follow the acts of good men, the Smritis have commanded the Hindus in unmistakable terms not to follow even gods in their good deeds, if they are contrary to Shruti, Smriti and sadachar. This may sound to be most extraordinary, most perverse, but the fact remains that it is an injunction issued to the Hindus by their Shastras.

## 22.17

Reason and morality are the two most powerful weapons in the armoury of a reformer. To deprive him of the use of these weapons is to disable him for action. How are you going to break up caste if people are not free to consider whether it accords with reason? How are you going to break up caste if people are not free to consider whether it accords with morality? The wall built around caste is impregnable, and the material of which it is built contains none of the combustible stuff of reason and morality. Add to this the fact that inside this wall stands the army of Brahmins who form the intellectual class, Brahmins who are the natural leaders of the Hindus, Brahmins who are there not as mere mercenary soldiers but as an army fighting for its homeland, and you will get an idea why I think that the breaking up of caste among the Hindus is well-nigh impossible. At any rate, it would take ages before a breach is made.

## 22.18

But whether the doing of the deed takes time or whether it can be done quickly, you must not forget that if you wish to bring about a breach in the system, then you have got to apply the dynamite to the Vedas and the Shastras, which deny any part to reason; to the Vedas and Shastras, which deny any part to morality. You must destroy the religion of the Shrutis and the Smritis. Nothing else will avail. This is my considered view of the matter.

# 23

## 23.1

Some may not understand what I mean by the destruction of religion, some may find the idea revolting to them, and some may find it revolutionary. Let me, therefore, explain my position. I do not know whether you draw a distinction between principles and rules. But I do. Not only do I make a distinction, but I say that this distinction is real and important. Rules are practical; they are habitual ways of doing things according to prescription. But principles are intellectual; they are useful methods of judging things. Rules seek to tell an agent just what course of action to pursue. Principles do not prescribe a specific course of action. Rules, like cooking recipes, do tell just what to do and how to do it. A principle, such as that of justice, supplies a main heading by reference to which he is to consider the bearings of his desires and purposes; it guides him in his thinking by suggesting to him the important consideration which he should bear in mind.

## 23.2

This difference between rules and principles makes the acts done in pursuit of them different in quality and in content. Doing what is said to be good by virtue of a rule and doing good in the light of a principle are two different things. The principle may be wrong, but the act is conscious and responsible. The rule may be right, but the act is mechanical. A religious act may not be a correct act, but must at least be a responsible act. To permit this responsibility, religion must mainly be a matter of principles only. It cannot be a matter of rules. The moment it degenerates into rules, it ceases to be religion, as it kills the responsibility which is the essence of a truly religious act.

## 23.3

What is this Hindu religion? Is it a set of principles, or is it a code of rules? Now, the Hindu religion, as contained in the Vedas and the Smritis, is nothing but a mass of sacrificial, social, political and sanitary rules and regulations, all mixed up. What is called religion by the Hindus is nothing but a multitude of commands and prohibitions. Religion, in the sense of spiritual principles, truly universal, applicable to all races, to all countries, to all times, is not to be found in them; and if it is, it does not form the governing part of a Hindu's life. That for a Hindu, dharma means commands and prohibitions, is clear from the way the word dharma is used in the Vedas and the Smritis and understood by the commentators. The word dharma, as used in the Vedas, in most cases, means religious ordinances or rites. Even Jaimini, in his *Purva Mimamsa,* defines dharma as "a desirable goal or result that is indicated by injunctive (Vedic) passages."

## 23.4

To put it in plain language, what the Hindus call religion is really law, or at best, legalised class-ethics. Frankly, I refuse to call this code of ordinances as religion. The first evil of such a code of ordinances, misrepresented to the people as religion, is that it tends to deprive moral life of freedom and spontaneity and to reduce it (for the conscientious, at any rate) to a more or less anxious and servile conformity to externally imposed rules. Under it, there is no loyalty to ideals; there is only conformity to commands.

## 23.5

But the worst evil of this code of ordinances is that the laws it contains must be the same yesterday, today and forever. They are iniquitous in that they are not the same for one class as for another. But this iniquity is made perpetual in that they are prescribed to be the same for all generations. The objectionable part of such a scheme is not that they are made by certain persons called prophets or law-givers. The objectionable part is that this code has been invested with the character of finality and fixity. Happiness notoriously varies with the conditions and circumstances of a person, as well as with the conditions of different people and epochs. That being the case, how can humanity endure this code of eternal laws, without being cramped and without being crippled?

## 23.6

I have, therefore, no hesitation in saying that such a religion must be destroyed, and I say, there is nothing irreligious in working for the destruction of such a religion. Indeed, I hold that it is your bounden duty to tear off the mask, to remove the misrepresentation that is caused by misnaming this law as religion. This is an essential step for you. Once you clear the minds of the people of this misconception and enable them to realise that what they are told is religion is not religion, but that it is really law, you will be in a position to urge its amendment or abolition.

## 23.7

So long as people look upon it as religion, they will not be ready for a change, because the idea of religion is generally speaking not associated with the idea of change. But the idea of law is associated with the idea of change, and when people come to know that what is called religion is really law, old and archaic, they will be ready for a change, for people know and accept that law can be changed.

# 24

## 24.1

While I condemn a religion of rules, I must not be understood to hold the opinion that there is no necessity for a religion. On the contrary, I agree with Burke when he says that "True religion is the foundation of society, the basis on which all true Civil Government rests, and both their sanction." Consequently, when I urge that these ancient rules of life be annulled, I am anxious that their place shall be taken by a religion of principles, which alone can lay claim to being a true religion. Indeed, I am so convinced of the necessity of religion that I feel I ought to tell you in outline what I regard as necessary items in this religious reform. The following, in my opinion, should be the cardinal items in this reform:

1. There should be one and only one standard book of the Hindu religion, acceptable to all Hindus and recognised by all Hindus. This, of course, means that all other books of the Hindu religion, such as the Vedas, Shastras and Puranas, which are treated as sacred and authoritative, must, by law, cease to be so, and the preaching of any doctrine, religious or social, contained in these books should be penalised.

2. It would be better if the priesthood among Hindus were abolished. But as this seems to be impossible, the priesthood must at least cease to be hereditary. Every person who professes to be a Hindu must be eligible to be a priest. It should be provided by law that no Hindu shall be entitled to be a priest unless he has passed an examination prescribed by the state and holds a *sanad* from the state permitting him to practise.

3. No ceremony performed by a priest who does not hold a sanad shall be deemed to be valid in law, and it should be made penal for a person who has no sanad to officiate as a priest.

4. A priest should be the servant of the state and should be subject to the disciplinary action of the state in the matter of his

morals, beliefs and worship, in addition to his being subject, along with other citizens, to the ordinary law of the land.

5. The number of priests should be limited by law according to the requirements of the state, as is done in the case of the ICS [Indian Civil Service].

## 24.2

To some, this may sound radical. But to my mind, there is nothing revolutionary in this. Every profession in India is regulated. Engineers must show proficiency, doctors must show proficiency, lawyers must show proficiency before they are allowed to practise their professions. During the whole of their career, they must not only obey the law of the land, civil as well as criminal, but they must also obey the special code of morals prescribed by their respective professions. The priest's is the only profession where proficiency is not required. The profession of a Hindu priest is the only profession which is not subject to any code.

## 24.3

Mentally, a priest may be an idiot; physically, a priest may be suffering from a foul disease such as syphilis or gonorrhoea; morally, he may be a wreck. But he is fit to officiate at solemn ceremonies, to enter the *sanctum sanctorum* of a Hindu temple and to worship the Hindu god. All this becomes possible among the Hindus because for a priest, it is enough to be born in a priestly caste. The whole thing is abominable and is due to the fact that the priestly class among Hindus is subject neither to law nor to morality. It recognises no duties. It knows only of rights and privileges. It is a pest which divinity seems to have let loose on the masses for their mental and moral degradation.

## 24.4

The priestly class must be brought under control by some such legislation as I have outlined above. This will prevent it from doing mischief and from misguiding people. It will democratise it by throwing it open to everyone. It will certainly help to kill

Brahminism and will also help to kill caste, which is nothing but Brahminism incarnate. Brahminism is the poison which has spoiled Hinduism. You will succeed in saving Hinduism if you kill Brahminism. There should be no opposition to this reform from any quarter. It should be welcomed even by the Arya Samajists, because this is merely an application of their own doctrine of guna-karma.

## 24.5

Whether you do that or you do not, you must give a new doctrinal basis to your religion – a basis that will be in consonance with liberty, equality and fraternity; in short, with democracy. I am no authority on the subject. But I am told that for such religious principles as will be in consonance with liberty, equality and fraternity, it may not be necessary for you to borrow from foreign sources and that you could draw for such principles on the Upanishads. Whether you could do so without a complete remoulding, a considerable scraping and chipping off of the ore they contain, is more than I can say. This means a complete change in the fundamental notions of life. It means a complete change in the values of life. It means a complete change in outlook and in attitude towards men and things.

## 24.6

It means conversion; but if you do not like the word, I will say it means new life. But a new life cannot enter a body that is dead. New life can enter only into a new body. The old body must die before a new body can come into existence, and a new life can enter into it. To put it simply: the old must cease to be operative before the new can begin to enliven and to pulsate. This is what I meant when I said you must discard the authority of the Shastras and destroy the religion of the Shastras.

# 25

## 25.1

I have kept you too long. It is time I brought this address to a close. This would have been a convenient point for me to have stopped. But this would probably be my last address to a Hindu audience on a subject vitally concerning the Hindus. I would, therefore, like, before I close, to place before the Hindus, if they will allow me, some questions which I regard as vital and invite them seriously to consider the same.

## 25.2

In the first place, the Hindus must consider whether it is sufficient to take the placid view of the anthropologist that there is nothing to be said about the beliefs, habits, morals and outlooks on life which obtain among the different peoples of the world, except that they often differ; or whether it is not necessary to make an attempt to find out what kind of morality, beliefs, habits and outlook have worked best and have enabled those who possessed them to flourish, to grow strong, to people the earth and to have dominion over it. As is observed by Prof. Carver: "Morality and religion, as the organised expression of moral approval and disapproval, must be regarded as factors in the struggle for existence as truly as are weapons for offence and defence, teeth and claws, horns and hoofs, fur and feathers, plumage, beards and antlers. The social group, community, tribe or nation which develops an unworkable scheme of morality, or within which those social acts which weaken it and unfit it for survival habitually create the sentiment of approval, while those which would strengthen it and enable it to expand habitually create the sentiment of disapproval, will eventually be eliminated. Its habits of approval and disapproval handicap it as really as the possession of two wings on one side with none on the other would handicap a colony of flies. It would be as futile in one case as in the other to argue that one system was just as good as another."

## 25.3

Morality and religion, therefore, are not mere matters of likes and dislikes. You may dislike exceedingly a scheme of morality which, if universally practised within a nation, would make that nation the strongest nation on the face of the earth. Yet, in spite of your dislike, such a nation will become strong. You may like exceedingly a scheme of morality and an ideal of justice which, if universally practised within a nation, would make it unable to hold its own in the struggle with other nations. Yet, in spite of your admiration, this nation will eventually disappear. The Hindus must, therefore, examine their religion and their morality in terms of their survival value.

## 25.4

Secondly, the Hindus must consider whether they should conserve the whole of their social heritage, or select what is helpful and transmit to future generations only that much and no more. Prof John Dewey, who was my teacher and to whom I owe so much, has said: "Every society gets encumbered with what is trivial, with dead wood from the past and with what is positively perverse... As a society becomes more enlightened, it realises that it is responsible not to conserve and transmit the whole of its existing achievements, but only such as make for a better future society. Even Burke, in spite of the vehemence with which he opposed the principle of change embodied in the French Revolution, was compelled to admit that a State without the means of some change is without the means of its conservation. Without such means, it might even risk the loss of that part of the constitution which it wished the most religiously to preserve." What Burke said of a state applies equally to society.

## 25.5

Thirdly, the Hindus must consider whether they must not cease to worship the past as supplying their ideals. The baneful effects of this worship of the past are best summed up by Prof. Dewey when he says: "An individual can live only in the present. The present is not just something which comes after the past; much less something produced by it. It is what life is in, leaving the past behind it. The study of past products will not help us to understand the present. A knowledge of the past and its heritage is of great significance when it enters into the present, but not otherwise. And the mistake of making the records and remains of the past the main material of education is that it tends to make the past a rival of the present and the present a more or less futile imitation of the past." The principle, which makes little of the present act of living and growing, naturally looks upon the present as empty and upon the future as remote. Such a principle is inimical to progress and is a hindrance to a strong and steady current of life.

## 25.6

Fourthly, the Hindus must consider whether the time has not come for them to recognise that there is nothing fixed, nothing eternal, nothing sanatan; that everything is changing, that change is the law of life for individuals as well as for society. In a changing society, there must be a constant revolution of old values; and the Hindus must realise that if there must be standards to measure the acts of men, there must also be a readiness to revise those standards.

# 26

## 26.1

I have to confess that this address has become too lengthy. Whether this fault is compensated to any extent by breadth or depth is a matter for you to judge. All I claim is to have told you candidly my views. I have little to recommend them, but some study and a deep concern for your destiny. If you will allow me to say it, these views are the views of a man who has been no tool of power, no flatterer of greatness. They come from one, almost the whole of whose public exertion has been one continuous struggle for liberty for the poor and for the oppressed, and whose only reward has been a continuous shower of calumny and abuse from national journals and national leaders, for no other reason except that I refuse to join with them in performing the miracle – I will not say trick – of liberating the oppressed with the gold of the tyrant and raising the poor with the cash of the rich.

## 26.2

All this may not be enough to commend my views. I think they are not likely to alter yours. But whether they do or do not, the responsibility is entirely yours. You must make your efforts to uproot caste, if not in my way, then in your way.

## 26.3

I am sorry, I will not be with you. I have decided to change. This is not the place for giving reasons. But even when I am gone out of your fold, I will watch your movement with active sympathy, and you will have my assistance for what it may be worth. Yours is a national cause. Caste is no doubt primarily the breath of the Hindus. But the Hindus have fouled the air all over, and everybody is infected – Sikh, Muslim and Christian. You, therefore, deserve the support of all those who are suffering from this infection – Sikh, Muslim and Christian.

## 26.4

Yours is more difficult than the other national cause, namely, swaraj. In the fight for swaraj, you fight with the whole nation on your side. In this, you have to fight against the whole nation – and that too, your own. But it is more important than swaraj. There is no use having swaraj if you cannot defend it. More important than the question of defending swaraj is the question of defending the Hindus under the swaraj. In my opinion, it is only when Hindu society becomes a casteless society that it can hope to have strength enough to defend itself. Without such internal strength, swaraj for Hindus may turn out to be only a step towards slavery. Goodbye, and good wishes for your success.

# Castes in India: Their Mechanism, Genesis and Development

Paper presented at an Anthropology Seminar taught by Dr. A. A. Goldenweiser, Columbia University, on 9th May 1916.

Text first printed in The Indian Antiquary, Vol. XLVI (May 1917)

1. Many of us, I dare say, have witnessed local, national or international expositions of material objects that make up the sum total of human civilisation. But few can entertain the idea of there being such a thing as an exposition of human institutions. Exhibition of human institutions is a strange idea; some might call it the wildest of ideas. But as students of Ethnology, I hope you will not be hard on this innovation, for it is not so, and to you at least it should not be strange.

2. You all have visited, I believe, some historic place like the ruins of Pompeii and listened with curiosity to the history of the remains as it flowed from the glib tongue of the guide. In my opinion, a student of Ethnology, in one sense at least, is much like the guide. Like his prototype, he holds up (perhaps with more seriousness and desire of self-instruction) the social institutions to view, with all the objectiveness humanly possible, and inquires into their origin and function.

3. Most of our fellow students in this seminar, which concerns itself with primitive versus modern society, have ably acquitted themselves along these lines by giving lucid expositions of the various institutions, modern or primitive, in which they are interested. It is my turn now, this evening, to entertain you, as best I can, with a paper on "*Castes in India*: Their Mechanism, Genesis and Development."

4. I need hardly remind you of the complexity of the subject I intend to handle. Subtler minds and abler pens than mine have been brought to the task of unravelling the mysteries of Caste; but unfortunately, it still remains in the domain of the "unexplained," not to say of the "un-understood." I am quite alive to the complex intricacies of a hoary institution like caste, but I am not so

pessimistic as to relegate it to the region of the unknowable, for I believe it can be known. The caste problem is a vast one, both theoretically and practically. Practically, it is an institution that portends tremendous consequences. It is a local problem, but one capable of much wider mischief, for "as long as caste in India does exist, Hindus will hardly intermarry or have any social intercourse with outsiders; and if Hindus migrate to other regions on earth, Indian caste would become a world problem." Theoretically, it has defied a great many scholars who have taken upon themselves, as a labour of love, to dig into its origin. Such being the case, I cannot treat the problem in its entirety. Time, space and acumen, I am afraid, would all fail me if I attempted to do otherwise than limit myself to a phase of it, namely, the genesis, mechanism and spread of the caste system. I will strictly observe this rule and will dwell on extraneous matters only when it is necessary to clarify or support a point in my thesis.

5. To proceed with the subject. According to well-known ethnologists, the population of India is a mixture of Aryans, Dravidians, Mongolians and Scythians. All these stocks of people came into India from various directions and with various cultures, centuries ago, when they were in a tribal state. They all, in turn, elbowed their entry into the country by fighting with their predecessors and, after a stomachful of it, settled down as peaceful neighbours. Through constant contact and mutual intercourse, they evolved a common culture that superseded their distinctive cultures. It may be granted that there has not been a thorough amalgamation of the various stocks that make up the peoples of India, and to a traveller from within the boundaries of India, the East presents a marked contrast in physique and even in colour to the West, as does the South to the North. But amalgamation can never be the sole criterion of homogeneity as predicated of any people. Ethnically, all people are heterogeneous. It is the unity of culture that is the basis of homogeneity. Taking this for granted, I venture to say that there is no country that can rival the Indian Peninsula with respect to the unity of its culture. It has not only a geographic unity, but it has, over and above all, a deeper and a much more fundamental unity – the indubitable cultural unity

that covers the land from end to end. But it is because of this homogeneity that caste becomes a problem so difficult to explain. If the Hindu society were a mere federation of mutually exclusive units, the matter would be simple enough. But caste is a parcelling of an already homogeneous unit, and the explanation of the genesis of caste is the explanation of this process of parcelling.

6. Before launching into our field of enquiry, it is better to advise ourselves regarding the nature of a caste. I will, therefore, draw upon a few of the best students of caste for their definitions of it:

(1) Mr. Senart, a French authority, defines a caste as "a close corporation, in theory, at any rate, rigorously hereditary: equipped with a certain traditional and independent organisation, including a chief and a council, meeting on occasion in assemblies of more or less plenary authority and joining together at certain festivals: bound together by common occupations, which relate more particularly to marriage and to food and to questions of ceremonial pollution and ruling its members by the exercise of jurisdiction, the extent of which varies, but which succeeds in making the authority of the community more felt by the sanction of certain penalties and, above all, by final irrevocable exclusion from the group."

(2) Mr. Nesfield defines a caste as "a class of the community which disowns any connection with any other class and can neither intermarry nor eat nor drink with any but persons of their own community."

(3) According to Sir H. Risley, "A caste may be defined as a collection of families or groups of families bearing a common name which usually denotes or is associated with specific occupation, claiming common descent from a mythical ancestor, human or divine, professing to follow the same professional callings and are regarded by those who are competent to give an opinion as forming a single homogeneous community."

(4) Dr Ketkar defines caste as "a social group having two characteristics: (i) membership is confined to those who are born of members and includes all persons so born; (ii) the members are forbidden by an inexorable social law to marry outside the group."

7. To review these definitions is of great importance for our purpose. It will be noticed that, taken individually, the definitions of three of the writers include too much or too little: none is complete or correct by itself, and all have missed the central point in the mechanism of the caste system. Their mistake lies in trying to define caste as an isolated unit by itself and not as a group within and with definite relations to the system of caste as a whole. Yet collectively, all of them are complementary to one another, each one emphasising what has been obscured in the other. By way of criticism, therefore, I will take only those points common to all castes in each of the above definitions, which are regarded as peculiarities of caste and evaluate them as such.

8. To start with Mr. Senart. He draws attention to the "idea of pollution" as a characteristic of caste. With regard to this point, it may be safely said that it is by no means a peculiarity of caste as such. It usually originates in priestly ceremonialism and is a particular case of the general belief in purity. Consequently, its necessary connection with caste may be completely denied without damaging the working of caste. The "idea of pollution" has been attached to the institution of caste, only because the caste that enjoys the highest rank is the priestly caste, while we know that the priest and purity are old associates. We may, therefore, conclude that the "idea of pollution" is a characteristic of caste only in so far as caste has a religious flavour.

9. Mr. Nesfield, in his way, dwells on the absence of messing with those outside the caste as one of its characteristics. In spite of the newness of the point, we must say that Mr. Nesfield has mistaken the effect for the cause. Caste, being a self-enclosed unit, naturally limits social intercourse, including messing, etc., to members within it. Consequently, this absence of messing with outsiders is not due to positive prohibition, but is a natural result of caste, i.e., exclusiveness. No doubt this absence of messing, originally due to exclusiveness, acquired the prohibitory character of a religious injunction, but it may be regarded as a later growth. Sir H. Risley makes no new point deserving of special attention.

10. We now pass on to the definition of Dr. Ketkar, who has done much for the elucidation of the subject. Not only is he a

native, but he has also brought a critical acumen and an open mind to bear on his study of caste. His definition merits consideration, for he has defined caste in its relation to a system of castes, and has concentrated his attention only on those characteristics which are absolutely necessary for the existence of a caste within a system, rightly excluding all others as being secondary or derivative in character. With respect to his definition, it must, however, be said that in it there is a slight confusion of thought, lucid and clear as it otherwise is. He speaks of the *Prohibition of Intermarriage* and *Membership by Autogeny* as the two characteristics of caste. I submit that these are but two aspects of one and the same thing and not two different things as Dr. Ketkar supposes them to be. If you prohibit intermarriage, the result is that you limit membership to those born within the group. Thus, the two are the obverse and the reverse sides of the same medal.

11. This critical evaluation of the various characteristics of caste leaves no doubt that prohibition, or rather the absence of intermarriage – endogamy, to be concise – is the only one that can be called the essence of caste when rightly understood. But some may deny this on abstract anthropological grounds, for there exist endogamous groups without giving rise to the problem of caste. In a general way, this may be true, as endogamous societies, culturally different, making their abode in localities more or less removed and having little to do with each other, are a physical reality.

The Negroes and the Whites and the various tribal groups that go by name of American Indians in the United States may be cited as more or less appropriate illustrations in support of this view. But we must not confuse matters, for in India, the situation is different. As pointed out before, the people of India form a homogeneous whole. The various races of India occupying definite territories have more or less fused into one another and do possess cultural unity, which is the only criterion of a homogeneous population. Given this homogeneity as a basis, caste becomes a problem altogether new in character and wholly absent in the situation constituted by the mere propinquity of endogamous social or tribal groups. Caste in India means an artificial chopping off of the population into fixed and definite units, each one prevented from fusing into another through the custom of endogamy. Thus, the conclusion is inevitable that *Endogamy is the only characteristic that is peculiar to caste,* and if we succeed in showing how endogamy is maintained, we shall practically have proved the genesis and also the mechanism of caste.

12. It may not be quite easy for you to anticipate why I regard endogamy as a key to the mystery of the caste system. Not to strain your imagination too much, I will proceed to give you my reasons for it.

13. It may also not be out of place to emphasise at this moment that no civilised society of today presents more survivals of primitive times than does the Indian society. Its religion is essentially primitive, and its tribal code, in spite of the advance of time and civilisation, operates in all its pristine vigour even today. One of these primitive survivals, to which I wish particularly to draw your attention, is the *Custom of Exogamy*. The prevalence of exogamy in the primitive worlds is a fact too well-known to need any explanation. With the growth of history, however, exogamy has lost its efficacy, and excepting the nearest blood-kins, there is usually no social bar restricting the field of marriage. But regarding the people of India, the law of exogamy is a positive injunction even today. Indian society still savours of the clan system, even though there are no clans; and this can be easily seen from the law of matrimony which centres round the principle of exogamy, for it is not that Sapindas (blood-kins) cannot marry, but a marriage even between Sagotras (of the same class) is regarded as a sacrilege.

14. Nothing is, therefore, more important for you to remember than the fact that endogamy is foreign to the people of India. The various Gotras of India are and have been exogamous; so are the other groups with totemic organisation. It is no exaggeration to say that with the people of India, exogamy is a creed and none dare infringe it, so much so that, in spite of the endogamy of the castes within them, exogamy is strictly observed and that there are more rigorous penalties for violating exogamy than there are for violating endogamy. You will, therefore, readily see that with exogamy as the rule, there could be no caste, for exogamy means fusion. But we have castes; consequently, in the final analysis creation of castes, so

far as India is concerned, means the superposition of endogamy on exogamy. However, in an originally exogamous population, an easy working out of endogamy (which is equivalent to the creation of caste) is a grave problem, and it is in the consideration of the means utilised for the preservation of endogamy against exogamy that we may hope to find the solution to our problem.

15. *Thus the superposition of endogamy on exogamy means the creation of caste.* But this is not an easy affair. Let us take an imaginary group that desires to make itself into a caste and analyse what means it will have to adopt to make itself endogamous. If a group desires to make itself endogamous, a formal injunction against intermarriage with outside groups will be of no avail, especially if, prior to the introduction of endogamy, exogamy had been the rule in all matrimonial relations. Again, there is a tendency in all groups lying in close contact with one another to assimilate and amalgamate and thus consolidate into a homogeneous society. If this tendency is to be strongly counteracted in the interest of caste formation, it is absolutely necessary to circumscribe a circle outside which people should not contract marriages.

16. Nevertheless, this encircling to prevent marriages from without creates problems from within, which are not very easy to solve. Roughly speaking, in a normal group, the two sexes are more or less evenly distributed, and generally speaking, there is an equality between those of the same age. The equality is, however, never quite realised in actual societies. At the same time, to the group that is desirous of making itself into a caste, the maintenance of equality between the sexes becomes the ultimate goal, for without it, endogamy can no longer subsist. In other words, if endogamy is to be preserved, conjugal rights from within have to be provided for; otherwise, members of the group will be driven out of the circle to take care of themselves in any way they can. But in order that the conjugal rights be provided for from within, it is absolutely necessary to maintain a numerical equality between the marriageable units of the two sexes within the group desirous of making itself into a caste. It is only through the maintenance of such an equality that the necessary endogamy of the group can be kept intact, and a very large disparity is sure to break it.

17. *The problem of caste, then, ultimately resolves itself into one of repairing the disparity between the marriageable units of the two sexes within it.* Left to nature, the much-needed parity between the units can be realised only when a couple dies simultaneously. But this is a rare contingency. The husband may die before the wife and create a *surplus woman*, who must be disposed of, else, through intermarriage, she will violate the endogamy of the group. In like manner, the husband may survive, his wife and be a *surplus man*, whom the group, while it may sympathise with him for the sad bereavement, has to dispose of, else he will marry outside the caste and will break the endogamy. Thus, both the *surplus man* and the *surplus woman* constitute a menace to the caste if not taken care of, for not finding suitable partners inside their prescribed circle (and left to themselves they cannot find any, for if the matter be not regulated there can only be just enough pairs to go round), very likely they will transgress the boundary, marry outside and import offspring that is foreign to the caste.

18. Let us see what our imaginary group is likely to do with this *surplus man* and *surplus woman*. We will first take up the case of the surplus woman. She can be disposed of in two different ways so as to preserve the endogamy of the caste.

19. First: burn her on the funeral pyre of her deceased husband and get rid of her. This, however, is rather an impracticable way of solving the problem of sex disparity. In some cases, it may work; in others, it may not. Consequently, every surplus woman cannot thus be disposed of, because it is an easy solution but a hard realisation. And so, the *surplus woman* (= widow), if not disposed of, remains in the group, but in her very existence lies a double danger. She may marry outside the caste and violate endogamy, or she may marry within the caste and, through competition, encroach upon the chances of marriage that must be reserved for the potential brides in the caste. She is, therefore, a menace in any case, and something must be done to her if she cannot be burnt along with her deceased husband.

20. The second remedy is to enforce widowhood on her for the rest of her life. So far as the objective results are concerned, burning is a better solution than enforcing widowhood. Burning

the widow eliminates all the three evils that a *surplus woman* is fraught with. Being dead and gone, she creates no problem of remarriage either inside or outside the caste. But compulsory widowhood is superior to burning because it is more practicable. Besides being comparatively humane, it also guards against the evils of remarriage as does burning; but it fails to guard the morals of the group. No doubt, under compulsory widowhood, the woman remains, and just because she is deprived of her natural right of being a legitimate wife in future, the incentive to immoral conduct is increased. But this is by no means an insuperable difficulty. She can be degraded to a condition in which she is no longer a source of allurement.

21. The problem of the *surplus man* (= widower) is much more important and much more difficult than that of the surplus woman in a group that desires to make itself into a caste. From time immemorial, man, as compared with woman, has had the upper hand. He is a dominant figure in every group and of the two sexes has greater prestige. With this traditional superiority of man over woman, his wishes have always been consulted. Woman, on the other hand, has been an easy prey to all kinds of iniquitous injunctions, religious, social or economic. But man, as a maker of injunctions, is most often above them all. Such being the case, you cannot accord the same kind of treatment to a *surplus man* as you can to a *surplus woman* in a caste.

22. The project of burning him with his deceased wife is hazardous in two ways: first of all, it cannot be done, simply because he is a man. Secondly, if done, a sturdy soul is lost to the caste. There remain then only two solutions which can conveniently dispose of him. I say conveniently, because he is an asset to the group.

23. Important as he is to the group, endogamy is still more important, and the solution must assure both these ends. Under these circumstances, he may be forced or, I should say, induced, after the manner of the widow, to remain a widower for the rest of his life. This solution is not altogether difficult, for without any compulsion, some are so disposed as to enjoy self-imposed celibacy, or even to take a further step of their own accord and renounce the world and its joys. But, given human nature as it is, this solution

can hardly be expected to be realised. On the other hand, as is very likely to be the case, if the *surplus man* remains in the group as an active participator in group activities, he is a danger to the morals of the group. Looked at from a different point of view, celibacy, though easy in cases where it succeeds, is not so advantageous even then to the material prospects of the caste. If he observes genuine celibacy and renounces the world, he would not be a menace to the preservation of caste endogamy or caste morals, as he undoubtedly would be if he remained a secular person. But as an ascetic celibate, he is as good as burnt, so far as the material well-being of his caste is concerned. A caste, in order that it may be large enough to afford a vigorous communal life, must be maintained at a certain numerical strength. But to hope for this and to proclaim celibacy is the same as trying to cure atrophy by bleeding.

24. Imposing celibacy on the *surplus man* in the group, therefore, fails both theoretically and practically. It is in the interest of the caste to keep him as a Grihastha (one who raises a family), to use a Sanskrit technical term. But the problem is to provide him with a wife from within the caste. At the outset, this is not possible, for the ruling ratio in a caste has to be one man to one woman, and none can have two chances of marriage, for in a caste thoroughly self-enclosed, there are always just enough marriageable women to go round for the marriageable men. Under these circumstances, the *surplus man* can be provided with a wife only by recruiting a bride from the ranks of those not yet marriageable in order to tie him down to the group. This is certainly the best of the possible solutions in the case of the *surplus man*. By this, he is kept within the caste. By this means, numerical depletion through constant outflow is guarded against, and by this, endogamy and morals are preserved.

25. It will now be seen that the four means by which numerical disparity between the two sexes is conveniently maintained are: (1) burning the widow with her deceased husband; (2) compulsory widowhood – a milder form of burning; (3) imposing celibacy on the widower; and (4) wedding him to a girl not yet marriageable. Though, as I said above, burning the widow and imposing celibacy on the widower are of doubtful service to the group in its endeavour

to preserve its endogamy, all of them operate as *means*. But means, as forces, when liberated or set in motion, create an end. What then is the end that these means create? They create and perpetuate endogamy, while caste and endogamy, according to our analysis of the various definitions of caste, are one and the same thing. Thus, the existence of these means is identical with caste, and caste involves these means.

26. This, in my opinion, is the general mechanism of a caste in a system of castes. Let us now turn from these high generalities to the castes in Hindu society and inquire into their mechanism. I need hardly premise that there are a great many pitfalls in the path of those who try to unfold the past, and caste in India to be sure is a very ancient institution. This is especially true where there exist no authentic or written records or where the people, like the Hindus, are so constituted that to them writing history is a folly, for the world is an illusion. But institutions do live, though for a long time they may remain unrecorded, and as often as not, customs and morals are like fossils that tell their own history. If this is true, our task will be amply rewarded if we scrutinise the solution the Hindus arrived at to meet the problems of the *surplus man* and *surplus woman*.

27. Complex though it be in its general working, the Hindu society, even to a superficial observer, presents three singular uxorial customs, namely:

(i) *Sati* or the burning of the widow on the funeral pyre of her deceased husband. (ii) Enforced widowhood by which a widow is not allowed to remarry. (iii) Girl marriage.

In addition, one also notes a great hankering after *Sannyasa* (renunciation) on the part of the widower, but this may in some cases be due purely to psychic disposition.

28. So far as I know, no scientific explanation of the origin of these customs is forthcoming even today. We have plenty of philosophy to tell us why these customs were honoured, but nothing to tell us the causes of their origin and existence. *Sati* has been honoured (Cf. A. K. Coomaraswamy, "Sati: A Defence of the Eastern Woman" in the *British Sociological Review*, Vol. VI, 1913) because it is a "proof of the perfect unity of body and soul"

between husband and wife and of "devotion beyond the grave," because it embodied the ideal of wifehood, which is well expressed by Uma when she said, "Devotion to her Lord is woman's honour, it is her eternal heaven: and O Maheshvara," she adds with a most touching human cry, "I desire not paradise itself if thou are not satisfied with me!" Why compulsory widowhood is honoured, I know not, nor have I yet met with anyone who sang in praise of it, though there are a great many who adhere to it. The eulogy in honour of girl marriage is reported by Dr. Ketkar to be as follows: "A really faithful man or woman ought not to feel affection for a woman or a man other than the one with whom he or she is united. Such purity is compulsory not only after marriage, but even before marriage, for that is the only correct ideal of chastity. No maiden could be considered pure if she feels love for a man other than the one to whom she might be married. As she does not know to whom she is going to be married, she must not feel affection for any man at all before marriage. If she does so, it is a sin. So it is better for a girl to know whom she has to love before any sexual consciousness has been awakened in her" (*History of Caste in India,* 1909). Hence, girl marriage.

29. This high-flown and ingenious sophistry indicates why these institutions were honoured, but does not tell us why they were practised. My own interpretation is that they were honoured because they were practised. Anyone slightly acquainted with the rise of individualism in the 18th century will appreciate my remark. At all times, it is the movement that is most important; and the philosophies grow around it long afterwards to justify it and give it moral support. In like manner, I urge that the very fact that these customs were so highly eulogised proves that they needed eulogy for their prevalence. Regarding the question as to why they arose, I submit that they were needed to create the structure of caste, and the philosophies in honour of them were intended to popularise them, or to gild the pill, as we might say, for they must have been so abominable and shocking to the moral sense of the unsophisticated that they needed a great deal of sweetening. These customs are essentially of the nature of means, though they are represented as ideals.

But this should not blind us from understanding the *results* that flow from them. One might safely say that the idealisation of means is necessary and, in this particular case, was perhaps motivated to endow them with greater efficacy. Calling a means an end does no harm, except that it disguises its real character; but it does not deprive it of its real nature, that of a means. You may pass a law that all cats are dogs, just as you can call a means an end. But you can no more change the nature of means thereby than you can turn cats into dogs; consequently, I am justified in holding that, whether regarded as ends or as means, *Sati*, *enforced widowhood* and *girl marriage* are customs that were primarily intended to solve the problem of the *surplus man* and *surplus woman* in a caste and to maintain its endogamy. Strict endogamy could not be preserved without these customs, while caste, without endogamy is a fake.

30. Having explained the mechanism of the creation and preservation of caste in India, the further question as to its genesis naturally arises. The question of origin is always an annoying question, and in the study of caste, it is sadly neglected; some have connived at it, while others have dodged it. Some are puzzled as to whether there could be such a thing as the origin of caste and suggest that "if we cannot control our fondness for the word 'origin,' we should better use the plural form, viz., 'origins of caste.'" As for myself, I do not feel puzzled by the origin of caste in India, for, as I have established before, endogamy is the only characteristic of caste, and when I say *origin of caste,* I mean *the origin of the mechanism for endogamy.*

31. The atomistic conception of individuals in a society so greatly popularised – I was about to say vulgarised – in political orations is the greatest humbug. To say that individuals make up society is trivial; society is always composed of classes. It may be an exaggeration to assert the theory of class-conflict, but the existence of definite classes in a society is a fact. Their basis may differ. They may be economic or intellectual or social, but an individual in a society is always a member of a class. This is a universal fact, and early Hindu society could not have been an exception to this rule, and as a matter of fact, we know it was not. If we bear this generalisation in mind, our study of the genesis of caste would be

very much facilitated, for we have only to determine what was the class that first made itself into a caste, for class and caste, so to say, are next door neighbours, and it is only a span that separates the two. A caste is an Enclosed Class.

32. The study of the origin of caste must furnish us with an answer to the question – what is the class that raised this "enclosure" around itself? The question may seem too inquisitorial, but it is pertinent, and an answer to this will serve to elucidate the mystery of the growth and development of castes all over India. Unfortunately, a direct answer to this question is not within my power. I can answer it only indirectly. I said just above that the customs in question were current in the Hindu society. To be true to facts, it is necessary to qualify the statement, as it connotes the universality of their prevalence. These customs in all their strictness are obtainable only in one caste, namely the Brahmins, who occupy the highest place in the social hierarchy of the Hindu society; and as their prevalence in non-Brahmin castes is derivative, their observance is neither strict nor complete. This important fact can serve as a basis for an important observation. If the prevalence of these customs, in the non-Brahmin castes, is derivative, as can be shown very easily, then it needs no argument to prove what class is the father of the institution of caste. Why the Brahmin class should have enclosed itself into a caste is a different question, which may be left as an employment for another occasion. But the strict observance of these customs and the social superiority arrogated by the priestly class in all ancient civilisations are sufficient to prove that they were the originators of this "unnatural institution" founded and maintained through these unnatural means.

33. I now come to the third part of my paper regarding the question of the growth and spread of the caste system all over India. The question I have to answer is: How did the institution of caste spread among the rest of the non-Brahmin population of the country? The question of the spread of the castes all over India has suffered a worse fate than the question of genesis. And the main cause, as it seems to me, is that the two questions of spread and of origin are not separated. This is because of the common belief among scholars that the caste system has either been imposed

upon the docile population of India by a law-giver as a divine dispensation, or that it has grown according to some law of social growth peculiar to the Indian people.

34. I first propose to handle the law-giver of India. Every country has its law-giver, who arises as an incarnation (*avatar*) in times of emergency to set right a sinning humanity and give it the laws of justice and morality. Manu, the law-giver of India, if he did exist, was certainly an audacious person. If the story that he gave the law of caste be credited, then Manu must have been a dare-devil fellow, and the humanity that accepted his dispensation must be a humanity quite different from the one we are acquainted with. It is unimaginable that the law of caste was given. It is hardly an exaggeration to say that Manu could not have outlived his law, for what is that class that can submit to be degraded to the status of brutes by the pen of a man and suffer him to raise another class to the pinnacle? Unless he was a tyrant who held all the population in subjection, it cannot be imagined that he could have been allowed to dispense his patronage in this grossly unjust manner, as may be easily seen by a mere glance at his "Institutes."

I may seem hard on Manu, but I am sure my force is not strong enough to kill his ghost. He lives like a disembodied spirit and is appealed to, and I am afraid will yet live long. One thing I want to impress upon you is that Manu did not give the law of caste and that he could not do so. Caste existed long before Manu. He was an upholder of it and, therefore, philosophised about it, but certainly he did not and could not ordain the present order of Hindu society. His work ended with the codification of existing caste rules and the preaching of Caste Dharma. The spread and growth of the caste system is too gigantic a task to be achieved by the power or cunning of an individual or of a class. Similar in argument is the theory that the Brahmins created the caste. After what I have said regarding Manu, I need hardly say anything more, except to point out that it is incorrect in thought and malicious in intent.

The Brahmins may have been guilty of many things, and I dare say they were, but the imposing of the caste system on the non-Brahmin population was beyond their mettle. They may have helped the process by their glib philosophy, but they certainly could not have pushed their scheme beyond their own confines. To fashion society after one's own pattern! How glorious! How hard! One can take pleasure and eulogise its furtherance; but cannot further it very far. The vehemence of my attack may seem to be unnecessary; but I can assure you that it is not uncalled for. There is a strong belief in the mind of orthodox Hindus that the Hindu society was somehow moulded into the framework of the caste system and that it is an organisation consciously created by the *Shastras*. Not only does this belief exist, but it is being justified on the ground that it cannot but be good, because it is ordained by the *Shastras* and the *Shastras* cannot be wrong. I have urged so much on the adverse side of this attitude, not because the religious sanctity is grounded on a scientific basis, nor to help those reformers who are preaching against it. Preaching did not make the caste system; neither will it unmake it. My aim is to show the falsity of the attitude that has exalted religious sanction to the position of a scientific explanation.

35. Thus, the great man theory does not help us very far in solving the spread of castes in India. Western scholars, probably not much given to hero-worship, have attempted other explanations. The nuclei, round which have "formed" the various castes in India, are, according to them: (1) occupation; (2) survivals of tribal organisation, etc.; (3) the rise of new belief; (4) cross-breeding; and (5) migration.

36. The question may be asked whether these nuclei do not exist in other societies and whether they are peculiar to India. If they are not peculiar to India, but are common to the world, why is it that they did not "form" caste in other parts of this planet? Is it because those parts are holier than the land of the *Vedas*, or that the professors are mistaken? I am afraid that the latter is the truth.

37. In spite of the high theoretical value claimed by the several authors for their respective theories based on one or other of the above nuclei, one regrets to say that on close examination they are nothing more than filling illustrations – what Matthew Arnold means by "the grand name without the grand thing in it." Such are the various theories of caste advanced by Sir Denzil Ibbetson, Mr. Nesfield, Mr. Senart and Sir H. Risley. To criticise them in a lump would be to say that they are a disguised form of the *Petitio*

*Principii* of formal logic. To illustrate: Mr. Nesfield says that " function and function only... was the foundation upon which the whole system of castes in India was built up." But he may rightly be reminded that he does not very much advance our thought by making the above statement, which practically amounts to saying that castes in India are functional or occupational, which is a very poor discovery! We have yet to know from Mr. Nesfield why it is that an occupational group turned into an occupational caste? I would very cheerfully have undertaken the task of dwelling on the theories of other ethnologists, had it not been for the fact that Mr. Nesfield's is a typical one.

38. Without stopping to criticise those theories that explain the caste system as a natural phenomenon occurring in obedience to the law of disintegration, as explained by Herbert Spencer in his formula of evolution; or as natural as "the structural differentiation within an organism," to employ the phraseology of orthodox apologists; or as an early attempt to test the laws of eugenics – as all belonging to the same class of fallacy which regards the caste system as inevitable, or as being consciously imposed in anticipation of these laws on a helpless and humble population, I will now lay before you my own view on the subject.

39. We shall be well advised to recall at the outset that the Hindu society, in common with other societies, was composed of classes and the earliest known are (1) the Brahmins or the priestly class; (2) the Kshatriya, or the military class; (3) the Vaishya, or the merchant class; and (4) the Shudra, or the artisan and menial class. Particular attention has to be paid to the fact that this was essentially a class system, in which individuals, when qualified, could change their class, and therefore, classes did change their personnel. At some time in the history of the Hindus, the priestly class socially detached itself from the rest of the body of people and, through a closed-door policy, became a caste by itself. The other classes, being subject to the law of social division of labour, underwent differentiation, some into large, others into very minute groups. The Vaishya and Shudra classes were the original inchoate plasm, which formed the sources of the numerous castes of today. As the military occupation does not very easily lend itself to very

minute sub-division, the Kshatriya class could have differentiated into soldiers and administrators.

40. This subdivision of a society is quite natural. But the unnatural thing about these subdivisions is that they have lost the open-door character of the class system and have become self-enclosed units called castes. The question is: Were they compelled to close their doors and become endogamous, or did they close them of their own accord? I submit that there is a double line of answer: *Some closed the door; others found it closed against them*. The one is a psychological interpretation and the other is mechanistic, but they are complementary and both are necessary to explain the phenomena of caste-formation in its entirety.

41. I will first take up the psychological interpretation. The question we have to answer in this connection is: Why did these subdivisions or classes, if you please, industrial, religious or otherwise, become self-enclosed or endogamous? My answer is because the Brahmins were so. Endogamy or the closed-door system was a fashion in the Hindu society, and as it had originated from the Brahmin caste, it was wholeheartedly imitated by all the non-Brahmin subdivisions or classes, who, in their turn, became endogamous castes. It is "the infection of imitation" that caught all these subdivisions on their onward march of differentiation and has turned them into castes. The propensity to imitate is a deep-seated one in the human mind and need not be deemed an inadequate explanation for the formation of the various castes in India. It is so deep-seated that Walter Bagehot argues that, "We must not think of... imitation as voluntary, or even conscious. On the contrary, it has its seat mainly in very obscure parts of the mind, whose notions, so far from being consciously produced, are hardly felt to exist; so far from being conceived beforehand, are not even felt at the time. The main seat of the imitative part of our nature is our belief, and the causes predisposing us to believe this or disinclining us to believe that are among the obscurest parts of our nature. But as to the imitative nature of credulity, there can be no doubt" (*Physics and Politics*, 1915).

This propensity to imitate has been made the subject of a scientific study by Gabriel Tarde, who lays down three laws of imitation. One of his three laws is that imitation flows from the higher to the lower or, to quote his own words, "Given the opportunity, a nobility will always and everywhere imitate its leaders, its kings or sovereigns, and the people likewise, given the opportunity, its nobility" (*Laws of Imitation*, tr. by E. C. Parsons, 2nd edition). Another of Tarde's laws of imitation is that the extent or intensity of imitation varies inversely in proportion to distance, or in his own words, "The thing that is most imitated is the most superior one of those that are nearest. In fact, the influence of the model's example is efficacious inversely to its distance as well as directly to its superiority. Distance is understood here in its sociological meaning. However distant in space a stranger may be, he is close by, from this point of view, if we have numerous and daily relations with him and if we have every facility to satisfy our desire to imitate him. This law of the imitation of the nearest, of the least distant, explains the gradual and consecutive character of the spread of an example that has been set by the higher social ranks" (*Ibid*).

42. In order to prove my thesis – which really needs no proof – that some castes were formed by imitation, the best way, it seems to me, is to find out whether or not the vital conditions for the formation of castes by imitation exist in the Hindu society. The conditions for imitation, according to this standard authority, are: (1) that the source of imitation must enjoy prestige in the group and (2) that there must be "numerous and daily relations" among members of a group. That these conditions were present in India, there is little reason to doubt. The Brahmin is a semi-god and very nearly a demi-god. He sets up a mode and moulds the rest. His prestige is unquestionable and is the fountain-head of bliss and good. Can such a being, idolised by scriptures and venerated by the priest-ridden multitude, fail to project his personality on the suppliant humanity? Why, if the story be true, he is believed to be the very end of creation. Such a creature is worthy of more than mere imitation, but at least of imitation; and if he lives in an endogamous enclosure, should not the rest follow his example? Frail humanity! Be it embodied in a grave philosopher or a frivolous housemaid, it succumbs. It cannot be otherwise. Imitation is easy and invention is difficult.

43. Yet, another way of demonstrating the play of imitation in the formation of castes is to understand the attitude of non-Brahmin classes towards those customs which supported the structure of caste in its nascent days until, in the course of history, it became embedded in the Hindu mind and hangs there to this day without any support – for now it needs no prop but belief – like a weed on the surface of a pond. In a way, but only in a way, the status of a caste in the Hindu society varies directly with the extent of the observance of the customs of *Sati*, enforced widowhood and girl marriage. But observance of these customs varies directly with the distance (I am using the word in the Tardian sense) that separates the caste. Those castes that are nearest to the Brahmins have imitated all three customs and insist on the strict observance thereof. Those that are less near have imitated enforced widowhood and girl marriage; others, a little further off, have only girl marriage; and those furthest off have imitated only the belief in the caste principle. This imperfect imitation, I dare say, is due partly to what Tarde calls "distance" and partly to the barbarous character of these customs. This phenomenon is a complete illustration of Tarde's law and leaves no doubt that the whole process of caste-formation in India is a process of imitation of the higher by the lower.

At this juncture, I will turn back to support a former conclusion of mine, which might have appeared to you as too sudden or unsupported. I said that the Brahmin class first raised the structure of caste with the help of those three customs in question. My reason for that conclusion was that their existence in other classes was derivative. After what I have said regarding the role of imitation in the spread of these customs among the non-Brahmin castes, as means or as ideals, though the imitators have not been aware of it, they exist among them as derivatives; and if they are derived, there must have been prevalent one original caste that was high enough to have served as a pattern for the rest. But in a theocratic society, who could be the pattern but the servant of God?

44. This completes the story of those that were weak enough to close their doors. Let us now see how others were closed in as a result of being closed out. This I call the mechanistic process of the formation of caste. It is mechanistic because it is inevitable.

That this line of approach, as well as the psychological one, to the explanation of the subject has escaped my predecessors is entirely due to the fact that they have conceived caste as a unit by itself and not as one within a system of caste. The result of this oversight or lack of sight has been very detrimental to the proper understanding of the subject matter and, therefore, its correct explanation.

I will proceed to offer my own explanation by making one remark which I will urge you to bear constantly in mind. It is this: that *caste in the singular number is an unreality. Castes exist only in the plural number.* There is no such thing as a caste: There are always castes. To illustrate my meaning: while making themselves into a caste, the Brahmins, by virtue of this, created the non-Brahmin caste; or, to express it in my own way, while closing themselves in, they closed others out. I will clear my point by taking another illustration. Take India as a whole with its various communities designated by the various creeds to which they owe allegiance, to wit, the Hindus, Mohammedans, Jews, Christians and Parsis. Now, barring the Hindus, the rest within themselves are non-caste communities. But with respect to each other, they are castes. Again, if the first four enclose themselves, the Parsis are directly closed out, but are indirectly closed in. Symbolically, if Group A wants to be endogamous, Group B has to be so by sheer force of circumstances.

45. Now, apply the same logic to the Hindu society, and you have another explanation of the "fissiparous" character of caste, as a consequence of the virtue of self-duplication that is inherent in it. Any innovation that seriously antagonises the ethical, religious and social code of the caste is not likely to be tolerated by the caste, and the recalcitrant members of a caste are in danger of being thrown out of the caste and left to their own fate without having the alternative of being admitted into or absorbed by other castes. Caste rules are inexorable, and they do not wait to make nice distinctions between kinds of offence. Innovation may be of any kind, but all kinds will suffer the same penalty. A novel way of thinking will create a new caste, for the old ones will not tolerate it. The noxious thinker, respectfully called Guru (Prophet), suffers the same fate as the sinners in illegitimate love. The former creates a caste of the nature of a religious sect, and the latter a type of mixed

caste. Castes have no mercy for a sinner who has the courage to violate the code. The penalty is excommunication, and the result is a new caste.

It is not peculiar Hindu psychology that induces the excommunicated to form themselves into a caste; far from it. On the contrary, very often they have been quite willing to be humble members of some caste (higher by preference) if they could be admitted within its fold. But castes are enclosed units, and it is their conspiracy with clear conscience that compels the excommunicated to make themselves into a caste. The logic of this obdurate circumstance is merciless, and it is in obedience to its force that some unfortunate groups find themselves enclosed, because others, in enclosing themselves, have closed them out, with the result that new groups (formed on any basis obnoxious to the caste rules) by a mechanical law are constantly being converted into castes to a bewildering multiplicity. Thus is told the second tale in the process of caste formation in India.

46. Now, to summarise the main points of my thesis. In my opinion, there have been several mistakes committed by the students of caste, which have misled them in their investigations. European students of caste have unduly emphasised the role of colour in the caste system. Themselves impregnated by colour prejudices, they very readily imagined it to be the chief factor in the caste problem. But nothing can be farther from the truth, and Dr. Ketkar is correct when he insists that "All the princes, whether they belonged to the so-called Aryan race, or the so-called Dravidian race, were Aryas. Whether a tribe or a family was racially Aryan or Dravidian was a question which never troubled the people of India until foreign scholars came in and began to draw the line. The colour of the skin had long ceased to be a matter of importance" (*History of Caste.*)

Again, they have mistaken mere descriptions for explanation and fought over them as though they were theories of origin. There are occupational, religious, etc., castes, it is true, but it is by no means an explanation of the origin of caste. We have yet to find out why occupational groups are castes; but this question has never even been raised. Lastly, they have taken caste very lightly as though a breath had made it. On the contrary, caste, as I have explained it, is almost impossible to be sustained, for the difficulties that it involves are tremendous. It is true that caste rests on belief, but before belief comes to be the foundation of an institution, the institution itself needs to be perpetuated and fortified. My study of the caste problem involves four main points: (1) that, in spite of the composite make-up of the Hindu population, there is a deep cultural unity; (2) that caste is a parcelling into bits of a larger cultural unit; (3) that there was one caste to start with; and (4) that classes have become castes through imitation and excommunication.

47. Peculiar interest attaches to the problem of caste in India today; as persistent attempts are being made to do away with this unnatural institution. Such attempts at reform, however, have aroused a great deal of controversy regarding its origin, as to whether it is due to the conscious command of a Supreme Authority, or is an unconscious growth in the life of a human society under peculiar circumstances. Those who hold the latter view will, I hope, find some food for thought in the standpoint adopted in this paper. Apart from its practical importance, the subject of caste is an all-absorbing problem, and the interest aroused in me regarding its theoretical foundations has moved me to put before you some of the conclusions which seem to me well-founded, and the grounds upon which they may be supported.

I am not, however, so presumptuous as to think them in any way final, or anything more than a contribution to a discussion of the subject. It seems to me that the car has been shunted on the wrong lines, and the primary object of the paper is to indicate what I regard to be the right path of investigation, with a view to arriving at a serviceable truth. We must, however, guard against approaching the subject with a bias. Sentiment must be outlawed from the domain of science, and things should be judged from an objective standpoint. For myself, I shall find as much pleasure in a positive destruction of my own ideology as in a rational disagreement on a topic, which, notwithstanding many learned disquisitions, is likely to remain controversial forever. To conclude, while I am ambitious to advance a theory of caste, if it can be shown to be untenable, I shall be equally willing to give it up.

# Ranade, Gandhi & Jinnah

Address delivered during the 101st birthday celebrations of Mahadev Govind Ranade on 18th January 1943 at Gokhale Memorial Hall, Poona.

# Preface

The Deccan Sabha of Poona invited me to deliver an address on the 101st birthday of the late Justice Mahadev Govind Ranade, which it proposed to celebrate and which fell on 18th January 1943. I was not very willing to accept the invitation. For I knew that my views on social and political problems, a discussion of which could not be avoided in a discourse on Ranade, would not be very pleasing to the audience and even perhaps to the members of the Deccan Sabha. In the end, I accepted their invitation. At the time when I delivered the address, I had no intention of publishing it. Addresses delivered on anniversaries of great men are generally occasional pieces. They do not have much permanent value. I did not think that my address was an exception to this. But I have some troublesome friends who have been keen on seeing the whole of it in print and have been insisting upon it. I am indifferent to the idea. I am quite content with the publicity it has received, and I have no desire to seek more. At the same time, if there are people who think that it is worthy of being rescued from falling into oblivion, I do not see any reason for disappointing them.

The address as printed differs from the address as delivered in two respects. Section X of the address was omitted from the address as delivered to prevent the performance going beyond a reasonable time. Even without it, it took an hour and a half to deliver the address. This is one difference. The other difference lies in the omission of a large portion of Section VIII, which was devoted to a comparison of Ranade with Phule. For this omission, there are two reasons. In the first place, the comparison was not sufficiently full and detailed to do justice to the two men; in the second place, when the difficulties of finding enough paper compelled me to sacrifice some portion of the address, this appeared to be the best offering.

The publication of the address is taking place under peculiar circumstances. Ordinarily, reviews follow publication. In this case, the situation is reversed. What is worse is that the reviews have condemned the address in scathing terms. This is a matter primarily for the publishers to worry about. I am happy that the publisher knows the risk and he takes it. Nothing more need be said about it except that it supports the view taken by my friends that the address contains matter which is of more than ephemeral value. As for myself, I am not in the least perturbed by the condemnation of this address by the Press. What is the ground for its condemnation? And who has come forward to condemn it?

I am condemned because I criticised Mr. Gandhi and Mr. Jinnah for the mess they have made of Indian politics, and that in doing so, I am alleged to have shown towards them hatred and disrespect. In reply to this charge, what I have to say is that I have been a critic, and I must continue to be such. It may be I am making mistakes, but I have always felt that it is better to make mistakes than to accept guidance and direction from others or to sit silent and allow things to deteriorate. Those who have accused me of having been actuated by feelings of hatred forget two things. In the first place, this alleged hatred is not born of anything that can be called personal. If I am against them, it is because I want a settlement. I want a settlement of some sort, and I am not prepared to wait for an ideal settlement. Nor can I tolerate anyone on whose will and consent the settlement depends, to stand on dignity and play the Grand Moghul. In the second place, no one can hope to make any effective mark upon his time and bring the aid that is worth bringing to great principles and struggling causes if he is not strong in his love and his hatred. I hate injustice, tyranny, pompousness and humbug, and my hatred embraces all those who are guilty of them. I want to tell my critics that I regard my feelings of hatred as a real force. They are only the reflex of the love I bear for the causes I believe in, and I am in no wise ashamed of it. For these reasons, I tender no apology for my criticism of Mr. Gandhi and Mr. Jinnah, the two men who have brought India's political progress to a standstill.

The condemnation is by the Congress Press. I know the Congress Press well. I attach no value to its criticism. It has never refuted my arguments. It knows only how to criticise, rebuke and revile me for everything I do; and to misreport, misrepresent and pervert everything I say. Nothing that I do pleases the Congress Press. This animosity of the Congress Press towards me can, to my mind, not unfairly, be explained as a reflex of the hatred of the Hindus for the Untouchables. That their animosity has become personal is clear from the fact that the Congress Press feels offended for my having criticised Mr. Jinnah, who has been the butt and the target of the Congress for the last several years.

However strong and however filthy be the abuses which the Congress Press chooses to shower on me, I must do my duty. I am no worshipper of idols. I believe in breaking them. I insist that if I hate Mr. Gandhi and Mr. Jinnah – I dislike them, I do not hate them – it is because I love India more. That is the true faith of a nationalist. I have hopes that my countrymen will someday learn that the country is greater than the men, that the worship of Mr. Gandhi or Mr. Jinnah and service to India are two very different things and may even be contradictory of each other.

B. R. Ambedkar<br>
15th March 1943<br>
22, Prithvi Raj Road<br>
New Delhi

# Ranade, Gandhi and Jinnah

## I

I must tell you that I am not very happy over this invitation. My fear is that I may not be able to do justice to the occasion. When a year ago, the centenary of Ranade's birthday was celebrated in Bombay, the Right Honourable Srinivas Shastri was chosen to speak. For very many reasons, he was well qualified for performing the duty. He can claim to be a contemporary of Ranade for a part of his life. He had seen him at close range and was an eyewitness to the work to which Ranade devoted his life. He had the opportunity to judge him and compare him with his co-workers. He could, therefore, expound his views about Ranade with a sense of confidence and with intimacy born out of personal touch. He could cite an anecdote and illuminate the figure of Ranade before his audience. None of these qualifications are available to me. My connection with Ranade is of the thinnest. I had not even seen him.

There are only two incidents about Ranade which I can recall. First, relates to his death. I was a student in the first standard at the Satara High School. On 16th January 1901, the High School was closed, and we, boys, had a holiday. We asked why it was closed, we were told that because Ranade was dead. I was then about 9 years old. I knew nothing about Ranade, who he was, what he had done; like other boys, I was happy over the holiday and did not care to know who died. The second incident, which reminds me of Ranade, is dated much later than the first. Once, I was examining some bundles of old papers belonging to my father when I found in them a paper which purported to be a petition sent by the Commissioned and non-Commissioned officers of the Mahar Community to the Government of India against the orders issued in 1892 banning the recruitment of the Mahars in the Army. On inquiry, I was told that this was a copy of a petition which was drafted by Ranade to help the aggrieved Mahars obtain redress.

Beyond these two incidents, I have nothing to recall about Ranade. My knowledge about him is wholly impersonal. It is derived from what I have read about his work and what others have said about him. You must not expect me to say anything of a personal character which will either interest you or instruct you. I propose to say what I think of him as a public man in his days and his place in Indian Politics today.

## II

As you are well aware, there are friends of Ranade who do not hesitate to describe him as a great man, and there are others who, with equal insistence, deny him that place. Where does the truth lie? But this question must, I think, wait upon another, namely, is history the biography of great men? The question is both relevant as well as important. For, if great men were not the makers of history, there is no reason why we should take more notice of them than we do of cinema stars. Views differ. There are those who assert that, however great a man may be, he is a creature of Time – Time called him forth, Time did everything, he did nothing. Those who hold this view, in my judgement, wrongly interpret history.

There have been three different views on the causes of historical changes. We have had the Augustinian theory of history, according to which history is only an unfolding of a divine plan in which mankind is to continue through war and suffering until that divine plan is completed on the day of judgement. There is the view of Buckle, who held that history was made by Geography and Physics. Karl Marx propounded a third view. According to him, history was the result of economic forces. None of these three would admit that history is the biography of great men. Indeed, they deny man any place in the making of history. No one except theologians accepts the Augustinian theory of history. As to Buckle and Marx, while there is truth in what they say, their views do not represent the whole truth. They are quite wrong in holding that impersonal forces are everything and that man is no factor in the making of history. That impersonal forces are a determining factor cannot be denied. But that the effect of impersonal forces depends on man must also be admitted.

Flint may not exist everywhere. But where it does exist, it needs man to strike flint against flint to make fire. Seeds may not be found everywhere. But where they do exist, it needs man to ground it to powder and make it a delectable and nutritious paste and thereby lay the foundation of agriculture. There are many areas devoid of metals. But where they do exist, it needs a man to make instruments and machines which are the basis of civilisation and culture.

Take the case of social forces. Various tragic situations arise. One such situation is of the type described by Thayer in his biography of Theodore Roosevelt when he says:

"There comes a time in every sect, party or institution when it stops growing, its arteries harden, its young men see no visions, its old men dream no dreams; it lives on the past and desperately tries to perpetuate the past. In politics, when this process of petrifaction is reached, we call it Bourbonism, and the sure sign of the Bourbon is that, being unconscious that he is the victim of sclerosis, he sees no reason for seeking a cure. Unable to adjust himself to changed and new conditions, he falls back into the past as an old man drops into his worn-out arm-chair."

The other kind of situation is not one of decay but of destruction. The possibilities of it are always present whenever there is a crisis. The old ways, old habits and old thoughts fail to lift society and lead it on. Unless new ones are found, there is no possibility of survival. No society has smooth sailing. There are periods of decay and possibilities of destruction through which every society has to pass. Some survive, some are destroyed, and some undergo stagnation and decay. Why does this happen? What is the reason that some survive? Carlyle has furnished an answer. He puts in his characteristic way:

"No time need have gone to ruin, could it have found a great enough, a man wise and good enough; Wisdom to discern truly what the Time wanted, valour to lead it on to the right road thither, these are the salvation of any Time."

This seems to me to be quite a conclusive answer to those who deny man any place in the making of history. The crisis can be met by the discovery of a new way. Where there is no new way found, society goes under. Time may suggest possible new ways. But to step on the right one is not the work of Time. It is the work of man. Man, therefore, is a factor in the making of history and that environmental forces, whether impersonal or social, if they are the first, are not the last things.

## III

Who can be called a great man? If asked of military heroes such as Alexander, Attila, Caesar and Tamerlane, the question is not difficult to answer. The military men make epochs and effect vast transitions. They appal and dazzle their contemporaries by their resounding victories. They become great without waiting to be called great. As the lion is among the deer, so they are among men. But it is equally true that their permanent effect on the history of mankind is very small. Their conquests shrink, and even so great a General as Napoleon, after all his conquests, left France smaller than he found it. When viewed from a distance, they are seen to be only periodical, if necessary, incidents in the world's movement, leaving no permanent mark on the character of the society in which they live The details of their career and their moral may be interesting, but they do not affect society and form no leaven to transform or temper the whole.

The answer becomes difficult when the question is asked about a person who is not a military general. For it then becomes a question of tests, and different people have different tests.

Carlyle, the apostle of Hero Worship, had a test of his own. He laid it down in the following terms:

"But of great man especially, of him I will venture to assert that it is incredible he should have been other than true. It seems to me the primary foundation of him, this... No man adequate to do anything, but is first of all in right earnest about it; what I call a sincere man. I should say sincerity, a deep, great, genuine sincerity, is the first characteristic of all men in any way heroic."

Carlyle was, of course, particular in defining his test of sincerity in precise terms, and in doing so, he warned his readers by defining what his idea of sincerity was:

"Not the sincerity that calls itself sincere: ah no," he said, "that is a very poor matter indeed – a shallow, braggart, conscious sincerity; oftenest self-conceit mainly. The great man's sincerity is of the kind he cannot speak of, is not conscious of: nay, I suppose, he is conscious rather of insincerity; for what man can walk accurately by the law of truth for one day? No, the great man does not boast himself sincere, far from that; perhaps does not ask himself if he is so: I would say rather, his sincerity does not depend on himself; he cannot help being sincere!"

Lord Rosebery proposed another test when dealing with Napoleon – who was as great an Administrator as a General. In answering the question, Was Napoleon great? Rosebery used the following language:

If by 'great' be intended the combination of moral qualities with those of intellect, great he certainty was not. But that he was great in the sense of being extraordinary and supreme, we can have no doubt. If greatness stands for natural power, for predominance, for something human beyond humanity, then Napoleon was assuredly great. Besides that indefinable spark which we call genius, he represents a combination of intellect and energy which has never perhaps been equalled, never, certainly, surpassed."

There is a third test, suggested by the philosophers or, to be more accurate, by those who believe in divine guidance of human affairs. They have a different conception of what a great man is. To summarise the summary of their view, as given by Rosebery, a great man is launched into the world, as a great natural or supernatural force, as a scourge and a scavenger born to cleanse society and lead it on to the right path, who is engaged in a vast operation, partly positive, mainly negative, but all relating to social regeneration.

Which of these is the true test? In my judgement, all are partial and none is complete. Sincerity must be the test of a great man. Clemenceau once said that most statesmen are rogues. Statesmen are not necessarily great men, and obviously, these on whose experience he founded his opinion must have been those wanting in sincerity. Nonetheless, no one can accept that sincerity is the primary or the sole test. For sincerity is not enough. A great man must have sincerity. For it is the sum of all moral qualities without which no man can be called great. But there must be something more than mere sincerity in a man to make him great.

A man may be sincere, and yet he may be a fool, and a fool is the very antithesis of a great man. A man is great because he finds a way to save society in its hours of crisis. But what can help him find the way? He can do so only with the help of intellect. Intellect is the light. Nothing else can be of any avail. It is quite obvious that without the combination of sincerity and intellect, no man can be great. Is this enough to constitute a great man? At this stage, we must, I think, make a distinction between an eminent individual and a great man. For I am certain that a great man is something very different from an eminent individual.

Sincerity and intellect are enough to mark out an individual as being eminent compared to his fellows. But they are not enough to raise him to the dignity of a great man. A great man must have something more than what a merely eminent individual has. What must be that thing? Here comes the importance of the philosopher's definition of a great man. A great man must be motivated by the dynamics of a social purpose and must act as the scourge and the scavenger of society. These are the elements which distinguish an eminent individual from a great man and constitute his title deeds to respect and reverence.

## IV

Was Ranade a great man? He was, of course, great in his person. Vast in physique – he could have been called "Your Immense" as the Irish servant who could not pronounce Your Eminence used respectfully to call Cardinal Wiseman – his master. He was a man of sanguine temperament, of genial disposition and versatile in his capacity. He had sincerity, which is the sum of all moral qualities, and his sincerity was of the sort which was prescribed by Carlyle. It was not a conscious "braggart sincerity." It was the natural sincerity, a constitutional trait, and not an assumed air. He was not only big in his physique and in his sincerity, he was also big in intellect. Nobody can question that Ranade had the intellect of a high calibre. He was not merely a lawyer and a judge of the High Court, he was a first-class economist, a first-class historian, a first-class educationist and a first-class Divine. He was not a politician. Perhaps it is good that he was not. For if he had been, he might not have been a great man. As Abraham Lincoln said, politicians "are a set of men who have interests aside from the interests of the people and who, to say the most of them, are taken as a mass, at least one long step removed from honest men."

Ranade, though not a politician, was a profound student of politics. Indeed, it would be difficult to find in the history of India any man who could come up to Ranade in the width of his learning, the breadth of his wisdom and the length of his vision. There was no subject which he did not touch and in which he did not acquire profundity. His reading was on the scale of the colossal, and every inch, he was a scholar. He was great not merely by the standard of his time, but he was great – measured by any standard.

As I have said, no claim for being a great man can rest on the foundation of sincerity and intellect either singly or in combination. Ranade could not be called great if he had these two qualities and no more. His title to being a great man must rest upon the social purposes he served and on the way he served them. On that, there can be no doubt. Ranade is known more as a social reformer than as a historian, economist or educationist. His whole life is nothing but a relentless campaign for social reform. It is on his role as a social reformer that this title of being a great man rests. Ranade had both the vision and the courage which the reformer needs, and in the circumstances in which he was born, his vision was no smaller a virtue than his courage. That he developed a vision of the Prophet – I am using the word in the Jewish sense – cannot but be regarded as a matter of surprise if the time in which he was born is taken into account.

Ranade was born in 1842, some 24 years after the Battle of Kirkee, which brought the Maratha Empire to an end. The downfall of the Maratha Empire evoked different feelings among different people. There were men like Natu who served as accessories before the fact. There were some who played the part of accessories after the fact, inasmuch as they were happy that the cursed rule of the Brahmin Peshwa was brought to an end. But there can be no doubt that a large majority of the people of Maharashtra were stunned by the event. When the whole of India was enveloped by the advancing foreign horde and its people being subjugated piece by piece, here in this little corner of Maharashtra lived a sturdy race who knew what liberty was, who had fought for it, inch by inch, and established it over miles and miles. By the British conquest, they had lost what was to them a most precious possession. One can quite imagine how the best intellect of Maharashtra had its mind utterly confounded and its horizon fully and completely darkened. What could be the natural reaction to so great a catastrophe? Can it be other than resignation, defeatism and surrender to the inevitable? How did Ranade react? Very differently. He held out the hope that the fallen shall rise. Indeed, he developed a new faith on which this hope was founded. Let me quote his own words. He said:

"I profess implicit faith in two articles of my creed. This country of ours is the true land of promise. This race of ours is the chosen race."

He did not rest quiet by merely enunciating this new Mosaic Gospel of hope and confidence. He applied his mind to the question of the realisation of this hope. The first requisite was, of course, a dispassionate analysis of the causes of this downfall. Ranade realised that the downfall was due to certain weaknesses in the Hindu social system, and unless these weaknesses were removed, the hope could not be realised. The new gospel was, therefore, followed by a call to duty. That duty was no other than the duty to reform Hindu society. Social reform became, therefore, the one dominant purpose of his life. He developed a passion for social reform, and there was nothing he did not do to promote it. His methods included meetings, missions, lectures, sermons, articles, interviews, letters – all carried on with an unrelenting zeal. He established many societies. He founded many journals. But he was not content with this.

He wanted something more permanent, something more systematic for promoting the cause of social reform. So he founded the Social Conference, an all-India organisation which ran as an adjunct to the Indian National Congress. Year after year, the Conference met to discuss the social ills and to find ways of remedying them, and year after year, Ranade attended its annual sessions as though it were a pilgrimage and fostered the cause of social reform.

In fostering the cause of social reform, Ranade showed great courage. Many people of this generation will perhaps laugh at such a claim. Courting prison has become an act of martyrdom in India. It is regarded both as a patriotic act and also as an act of courage. Most people who would otherwise be beneath notice and in whose case it could rightly be said that they were scoundrels who had taken to politics as their last refuge, have, by going to prison, become martyrs and have acquired a name and fame which, to say the least, is quite astounding. There would be some substance in this view if prison life involved the rigours to which men like Tilak and those of his generation had been subjected.

Prison life today has lost all its terrors. It has become a mere matter of detention. Political prisoners are no longer treated as criminals. They are placed in a separate class. There are no hardships to suffer, there is no reputation to lose, and there is no privation to undergo. It calls for no courage. But even when prison life had, as in the time of Mr. Tilak, its rigours, the political prisoners could make no claim to greater courage than a social reformer. Most people do not realise that society can practise tyranny and oppression against an individual in a far greater degree than a government can. The means and scope that are open to society for oppression are more extensive than those that are open to the government, also they are far more effective.

What punishment in the penal code is comparable in its magnitude and its severity to excommunication? Who has greater courage – the social reformer who challenges society and invites upon himself excommunication, or the political prisoner who challenges the government and incurs a sentence of a few months or a few years imprisonment? There is also another difference which is often lost sight of in estimating the courage shown by the social reformer and the political patriot. When the social reformer challenges society, there is nobody to hail him a martyr. There is nobody even to befriend him. He is loathed and shunned. But when the political patriot challenges the government, he has the whole society to support him. He is praised, admired and elevated as the saviour. Who shows more courage – the social reformer who fights alone, or the political patriot who fights under the cover of a vast mass of supporters? It would be idle to deny that Ranade showed courage in taking up the cause of social reform. Indeed, he showed a high degree of courage. For let it be remembered that he lived in times when social and religious customs, however gross and unmoral, were regarded as sacrosanct, and when any doubt questioning their divine and moral basis was regarded not merely as heterodoxy, but as intolerable blasphemy and sacrilege.

## V

His path as a reformer was not smooth. It was blocked from many sides. The sentiments of the people whom he wanted to reform were deeply rooted in the ancient past. They held the belief that their ancestors were the wisest and the noblest of men, and the social system which they had devised was of the most ideal character. What appeared to Ranade to be the shames and wrongs of the Hindu society were to them the most sacred injunctions of their religion. This was the attitude of the common man.

The intelligentsia was divided into two schools – a school which was orthodox in its beliefs but unpolitical in its outlook, and a school which was modern in its beliefs but primarily political in its aims and objects. The former was led by Mr. Chiplunkar and the latter by Mr. Tilak. Both combined against Ranade and created as many difficulties for him as they could. They not only did the greatest harm to the cause of social reform, but as experience shows, they have done the greatest harm to the cause of political reform in India. The unpolitical or the orthodox school believed in the Hegelian view – it is a puzzle to me – namely, to realise the ideal and idealise the real. In this, it was egregiously wrong. The Hindu religious and social system is such that you cannot go forward to give its ideal form a reality because the ideal is bad; nor can you attempt to elevate the real to the status of the ideal because the real, i.e., the existing state of affairs, is worse than worse could be. This is no exaggeration.

Take the Hindu religious system or take the Hindu social system, and examine it from the point of social utility and social justice. It is said that religion is good when it is fresh from the mint. But the Hindu religion has been a bad coin to start with. The Hindu ideal of society as prescribed by the Hindu religion has acted as a most demoralising and degrading influence on Hindu society. It is Nietzschean in its form and essence. Long before Nietzsche was born, Manu had proclaimed the gospel which Nietzsche sought to preach. It is a religion which is not intended to establish liberty, equality and fraternity. It is a gospel which proclaims the worship of the superman – the Brahmin – by the rest of the Hindu society. It propounds that the superman and his class alone are born to live and to rule. Others are born to serve them, and to nothing more. They have no life of their own to live, and no right to develop their own personality. This has been the gospel of the Hindu religion.

Hindu philosophy, whether it is Vedanta, Sankhya, Nyaya or Vaishashika, has moved in its own circle without in any way affecting the Hindu religion. It has never had the courage to challenge this gospel. That Hindu philosophy that everything is Brahma remained only a matter of intellect. It never became a social philosophy. The Hindu philosophers had both their philosophy and their Manu held apart in two hands, the right not knowing what the left had. The Hindu is never troubled by their inconsistency. As to their social system, can things be worse? The caste system is in itself a degenerate form of the Chaturvarna, which is the ideal of the Hindu. How can anybody who is not a congenital idiot accept Chaturvarna as the ideal form of society? Individually and socially, it is a folly and a crime. One class and one class alone to be entitled to education and learning! One class and one class alone to be entitled to Arms! One class and one class alone to trade! One class and one class alone to serve! For the individual, the consequences are obvious. Where can you find a learned man who has no means of livelihood, who will not degrade his education? Where can you find a soldier with no education and culture who will use his arms to conserve and not to destroy? Where can you find a merchant with nothing but the acquisitive instinct to follow who will not descend to the level of the brute? Where can you find the servant who is not to acquire education, who is not to own arms, and who is not to possess other means of livelihood, to be a man as his Maker intended him to be? If baneful to the individual, it makes society vulnerable. It is not enough for a social structure to be good for fair weather. It must be able to weather the storm.

Can the Hindu caste system stand the gale and the wind of aggression? It is obvious that it cannot. Either for defence or for offence, a society must be able to mobilise its forces. With functions and duties exclusively distributed and immutably assigned, what way is there for mobilisation? Ninety per cent of the Hindus – Brahmins, Vaishyas and Shudras – could not bear arms under the Hindu social system. How can a country be defended if its army cannot be increased in the hour of its peril? It is not Buddha who, as is often alleged, weakened Hindu society by his gospel of non-violence. It is the Brahminic theory of Chaturvarna that has been responsible not only for the defeat but for the decay of Hindu society.

Some of you will take offence at what I have said about the demoralising effect of the Hindu socio-religious ideal on Hindu society. But what is the truth? Can the charge be denied? Is there any society in the world which has unapproachable, unshadowables and unseeables? Is there any society which has a population of criminal tribes? Is there a society in which there exist today primitive people, who live in jungles, who do not even know to clothe themselves? How many do they count in numbers? Is it a matter of hundreds, is it a matter of thousands? I wish they numbered a paltry few. The tragedy is that they have to be counted in millions, millions of Untouchables, millions of criminal tribes, millions of primitive tribes!! One wonders whether the Hindu civilisation is civilisation or infamy. This is about the ideal.

Turn now to the state of things as it existed when Ranade came on the scene. It is impossible to realise now the state of degradation they had reached when the British came on the scene, and with which the reformers like Ranade were faced. Let me begin with the condition of the intellectual class. The rearing and guiding of a civilisation must depend upon its intellectual class – upon the lead given by the Brahmins. Under the old Hindu Law, the Brahmin enjoyed the benefit of the clergy and could not be hanged even if he was guilty of murder, and the East India Company allowed him the privilege till 1817. That is no doubt because he was the salt of the Earth. Was there any salt left in him? His profession had lost all its nobility. He had become a pest. The Brahmin systematically preyed on society and profiteered in religion. The Puranas and Shastras, which lie manufactured in tons, are a treasure trove of sharp practices which the Brahmins employed to befool, beguile and swindle the common mass of poor, illiterate and superstitious Hindus. It is impossible in this address to give references to them.

I can only refer to the coercive measures which the Brahmins had sanctified as proper to be employed against the Hindus, to the encashment of their rights and privileges. Let those who want to know read the preamble to Regulation XXI of 1795. According to it, whenever a Brahmin wanted to get anything which could not be willingly got from his victim, he resorted to various coercive practices – lacerating his own body with knives and razors, or threatening to swallow some poison, were the usual tricks he practised to carry out his selfish purposes. There were other ways employed by the Brahmin to coerce the Hindus, which were as extraordinary as they were shameless. A common practice was the erection in front of the house of his victim of the koorh – a circular enclosure in which a pile of wood was placed; within the enclosure, an old woman was placed, ready to be burnt in the koorh if his object was not granted. The second device of such a kind was the placing of his women and children in the sight of his victim and threatening to behead them. The third was the dhurna – starving on the doorstep of the victim.

This is nothing. Brahmins had started making claims for the right to deflower the women of non-Brahmins. The practice prevailed in the family of the Zamorin of Calicut and among the Vallabhachari sect of Vaishnavas. What depths of degradation the Brahmins had fallen to! If, as the Bible says, the salt has lost its flavour, wherewith shall it be salted? No wonder the Hindu society had its moral bonds loosened to a dangerous point. The East India Company had, in 1819, to pass a Regulation (VII of 1819) to put a stop to this moral degeneracy. The preamble to the Regulation says that women were employed wholesale to entice and take away the wives or female children for purposes of prostitution, and it was common practice among husbands and fathers to desert their families and children. Public conscience there was none, and in the absence of conscience, it was futile to expect moral indignation against the social wrongs.

Indeed, the Brahmins were engaged in defending every wrong for the simple reason that they lived on them. They defended untouchability, which condemned millions to the lot of the helot. They defended caste, they defended female child marriage, and they defended enforced widowhood – the two great props of the caste system. They defended the burning of widows, and they defended the social system of graded inequality with its rule of hypergamy, which led the Rajputs to kill in their thousands the daughters that were born to them. What shame! What wrong! Can such a society show its face before civilised nations? Can such a society hope to survive? Such were the questions which Ranade asked. He concluded that on only one condition it could be saved – namely, rigorous social reform.

## VI

His greatest opponents, however, came from the political school of the intelligentsia. These politicals developed a new thesis. According to that thesis, political reform was to have precedence over social reform. The thesis was argued from platform to platform and was defended by eminent people like Mr. Justice Telang, a Judge of the Bombay High Court, with the consummate skill of an acute lawyer. The thesis caught the imagination of the people. If there was one single cause to which the blocking of the social reform movement could be attributed, it was this cry of political reform. The thesis is unsupportable, and I have no doubt that the opponents of Ranade were wrong and, in pursuing it, did not serve the best interests of the country. The grounds on which Mr. Justice Telang defended the politicians' thesis were, of course, logical. But he totally forgot that logic is not reason, and analogy is not argument. Neither did he have a correct understanding of the inter-relation between the "social" and the "political," which Ranade had.

Let us examine the reasons for the thesis. Those that were advanced were not very impressive. But I am prepared to meet the most impressive arguments that could be advanced. Even then, the thesis will not stand. The following strikes me as being the most impressive. In the first place, it could be said that we want political power first because we want to protect the rights of the people. This answer proceeds from a very frugal theory of government as was propounded by the American statesman Jefferson, according to whom politics was only an affair of policing by the State so that the rights of people were maintained without disturbance. Assume that the theory is a sound one. The question is, what is there for the State to police if there are no rights? Rights must exist before policing becomes a serious matter of substance. The thesis that political reform should precede social reform becomes, on the face of it, an absurd proposition, unless the idea is that the government is to protect those who have vested rights and to penalise those who have none.

The second ground that could be urged in support of the thesis is that they wanted political power because they wanted to confer on each individual certain fundamental rights by law and that such conferring of the political rights could not take place unless there was political power first obtained. This, of course, sounds very plausible. But is there any substance in it? The idea of fundamental rights has become a familiar one since their enactment in the American Constitution and in the Constitution framed by Revolutionary France. The idea of making a gift of fundamental rights to every individual is no doubt very laudable. The question is how to make them effective. The prevalent view is that once rights are enacted in a law, then they are safeguarded. This again is an unwarranted assumption.

As experience proves, rights are protected not by law but by the social and moral conscience of society. If the social conscience is such that it is prepared to recognise the rights which law chooses to enact, rights will be safe and secure. But if the fundamental rights are opposed by the community, no law, no parliament, no judiciary can guarantee them in the real sense of the word. What is the use of the fundamental rights to the Negroes in America, to the Jews in Germany, and to the Untouchables in India? As Burke said, there is no method found for punishing the multitude. Law can punish a single, solitary recalcitrant criminal. It can never operate against a whole body of people who are determined to defy it. Social conscience – to use the language of Coleridge – that calm, incorruptible legislator of the soul without whom all other powers would "meet in mere oppugnancy – is the only safeguard of all rights fundamental or non-fundamental."

The third argument of the politicals could be based on the right to self-government. That self-government is better than good government is a well-known cry. One cannot give it more value than one can give to a slogan, and all would like to be assured that self-government would also be a good government. There is no doubt that the politicals wanted good government, and their aim was to establish a democratic form of government. But they never stopped to consider whether a democratic form of government was possible. Their contention was founded on a series of fallacies. A democratic form of government presupposes a democratic form of society. The formal framework of democracy is of no value and would indeed be a misfit if there were no social democracy. The politicals never realised that democracy was not a form of government. It was essentially a form of society. It may not be necessary for a democratic society to be marked by unity, by community of purpose, by loyalty to public ends and by mutuality of sympathy. But it does unmistakably involve two things. The first is an attitude of mind, an attitude of respect and equality towards their fellows. The second is a social organisation free from rigid social barriers. Democracy is incompatible and inconsistent with isolation and exclusiveness, resulting in the distinction between the privileged and the unprivileged. Unfortunately, the opponents of Ranade were never able to realise the truth of this fact.

One may judge it by any test, and it will be found that the stand that Ranade took in this controversy and his plan of work were correct and fundamental to – if they were not the pre-requisites of – political reform. Ranade argued that there were no rights in the Hindu society which the moral sense of man could recognise. There were privileges and disabilities, privileges for a few and disabilities for the vast majority. Ranade struggled to create rights. Ranade wanted to vitalise the conscience of the Hindu society, which had become moribund as well as morbid. Ranade aimed to create a real social democracy, without which there could be no sure and stable politics. The conflict was between two opposing points of view, and it centred round the question of which is more important for the survival of a nation, political freedom or strong moral fibre. Ranade took the view that moral stamina was more important than political freedom. This was also the view of Lecky, the great historian who, after a careful and comparative study of history, came to the conclusion that:

"The foundation of a nation's strength and prosperity is laid in pure domestic life, in commercial integrity, in a high standard of moral worth and of public spirit, in a simple habits, in courage, uprightness and a certain soundness and moderation of judgement which springs quite as much from character as from intellect. If you would form a wise judgement of the future of a nation, observe carefully whether these qualities are increasing or decaying. Observe carefully what qualities count for most in public life. Is character becoming of greater or less importance? Are the men who obtain the highest posts in the nation men of whom, in private life, irrespective of party, competent judges speak with genuine respect? Are they of sincere convictions, consistent lives and indisputable integrity? It is by observing this current that you can best cast the horoscope of a nation."

Ranade was not only wise, but he was also logical. He told his opponents against playing the part of Political Radicals and Social Tories. In clear and unmistakable terms, he warned them, saying:

"You cannot be liberal by halves. You cannot be liberal in politics and conservative in religion. The heart and the head must go together. You cannot cultivate your intellect, enrich your mind, enlarge the sphere of your political rights and privileges and, at the same time, keep your hearts closed and cramped. It is an idle dream to expect men to remain enchained and enshackled in their own superstition and social evils, while they are struggling hard to win rights and privileges from their rulers. Before long, these vain dreamers will find their dreams lost."

Experience has shown that these words of Ranade have been true, even prophetic. Let those who deny this consider: Where are we today in politics, and why are we where we are? It is now 50 years since the National Congress was born. Its stewardship has passed hands, I won't say from the sane to the insane, or from realists to idealists, but from moderates to radicals. Where does the country stand today at the end of 50 years of political marching? What is the cause of this deadlock? The answer is simple. The cause of the deadlock is the absence of a communal settlement. Ask why is communal settlement is necessary for political settlement, and you realise the fundamental importance of the stand that Ranade took. For the answer to this question is to be found in the wrong social system, which is too undemocratic, too over-weighed in favour of the classes and against the masses, too class-conscious and too communally-minded. Political democracy would become a complete travesty if it were built upon its foundations. That is why nobody except the high-caste Hindus will agree to make it the case of a political democracy without serious adjustments. Well, some people may argue to their satisfaction that the deadlock is the creation of the British Government. People like to entertain thoughts which soothe them and which throw responsibility on others. This is the psychology of escapism. But it cannot alter the fact that it is the defects of the social system which have given rise to the communal problem and which have stood in the way of India getting political power.

Ranade's aim was to cleanse the old order, if not to build a new one. He insisted on improving the moral tone of Hindu society. If he had been heard and followed, the system would have at least lost its rigour and its rigidity. If it could not have avoided communal settlement, it would have made it easy. For his attempts, limited as they were, would have opened the way to mutual trust. But the politicals had developed a passion for political power which had so completely blinded them that they refused to see virtue in anything else. Ranade has had his revenge. Is not the grant of political safeguards a penalty for denying the necessity of social reform?

How much did Ranade achieve in the field in which he played so dominant a part? In a certain sense, the question is not very important. Achievement is never the true measure of greatness. "Alas," as Carlyle said, "we know very well that ideals can never be completely embodied in practice. Ideals must ever lie a very great way off; and we will right thankfully content ourselves with any not intolerable approximation thereto!" Let no man, as Schillar says, too querulously, "measure by a scale of perfection the meagre product of reality" in this poor world of ours. We will esteem him no wise man; we will esteem him a sickly, discontented, foolish man. And yet Ranade's record of achievement was not altogether bare.

The problems facing the then social reformers contained in the statement on social reform prepared by Rai Bahadur P. Anandcharly were five: (1) Early marriage; (2) Remarriages of widows; (3) Liberty for our countrymen to travel – or sojourn in foreign lands; (4) Women's rights of property; and (5) Education of women. Of this programme, he achieved a great part. If he did not achieve all, there were the odds against him, which should never be forgotten. A clever, a determined and an insincere intelligentsia came forward to defend orthodoxy and give battle to Ranade. The scenes were exciting, as exciting as those of a dread, grim battle. And battle it was. One cannot recall the spirit of the time when this controversy over social reform was raging in this country. It is not possible for decency to enter into the abuses that were hurled, the calumnies that were uttered, the strategies that were employed by the orthodox section against the social reformers. It is impossible to read the writing of those who supported orthodoxy in their opposition to the Age of Consent Bill without realising the depth of the degradation to which the so-called leaders of the peoples had fallen. The Bill aimed to punish a husband who would have sexual intercourse with his wife if she had not attained the age of 12. Could any sane man, could any man with a sense of shame, oppose so simple a measure? But it was opposed, and Ranade had to bear the brunt of the mad orthodoxy. Assuming that Ranade's achievements were small; who could take pride or exultation in his failure to achieve more? There was no cause for exultation. The decline of social reform was quite natural. The odium of social reform was too great. The appeal of political power too alluring. The result was that social reform found fewer and fewer adherents. In the course of time, the platform of the Social Reform Conference was deserted, and men flocked to the Indian National Congress. The politicians triumphed over the social reformers. I am sure that nobody will now allow that their triumph was a matter for pride. It is certainly a matter of sorrow. Ranade may not have been altogether on the winning side, but he was not on the wrong side and certainly never on the side of the wrong as some of his opponents were.

## VII

How does Ranade compare with others? Comparisons are always odious and unpleasant. At the same time, it is true that there is nothing more illuminating than comparisons. Of course, in making them, one must bear in mind that to be interesting and instructive, comparisons must be between those that are alike. Fortunately, there is a field for comparison. Ranade was a social reformer, and as a social reformer, he could be usefully compared with other social reformers. Particularly illuminating will be the comparison between Ranade and Jyotirao Phule. Phule was born in 1827 and died in 1890. Ranade was born in 1842 and died in 1901. Thus, Phule and Ranade were contemporaries, and both were among the foremost social reformers.

Some may perhaps demur to the wisdom of comparing Ranade with other politicians. This can only be on the ground that Ranade was not a politician. To say that Ranade was not a politician is to impose a very narrow and very restricted meaning upon the term politician. A politician does not merely trade in politics, but he also represents a particular faith, covering both the method as well as the metaphysics of politics. Ranade was the founder of a school of politics which was distinctive for its method as well as for metaphysics. Used in this sense, Ranade was a politician and could be usefully compared with other politicians. Comparisons of Ranade with social reformers and with politicians cannot but be illuminating, and there is enough material for such comparisons.

The question really is one of time and taste. Time will not permit any extensive comparison of Ranade being made with both social reformers as well as with politicians. I must really choose between comparing Ranade with social reformers or with politicians. This is a matter of taste. Left to myself, I would have preferred to use my available time to compare Ranade with Phule. For I regard social reform as more fundamental than political reform. Unfortunately, my taste is different from the taste of the audience, and I feel that in detaining the audience, I must be guided more by its likes and dislikes than my own. The ardour for social reform has cooled down. The craze for politics has held the Indian public in its grip. Politics has become an appetiser – a mastic such that the more one tastes it, the more one craves it. The task I am undertaking is a very unpleasant one, and if I venture upon it, it is only because it is my duty to expound fully, and the desire of the public to know truly, the value of Ranade's political philosophy and his place among politicians of today.

Who are the present-day politicians with whom Ranade is to be compared? Ranade was a great politician of his day. He must, therefore, be compared with the greatest of today. We have on the horizon of India two great men, so big that they could be identified without being named – Gandhi and Jinnah. What sort of history they will make may be a matter for posterity to tell. For us, it is enough that they do indisputably make headlines for the Press. They hold leading strings. One leads the Hindus, the other leads the Muslims. They are the idols and heroes of the hour. I propose to compare them with Ranade.

How do they compare with Ranade? It is necessary to make some observations upon their temperaments and methods, with which they have now familiarised us. I can give only my impressions of them, for what they are worth. The first thing that strikes me is that it would be difficult to find two persons who would rival them for their colossal egotism, to whom personal ascendancy is everything and the cause of the country a mere counter on the table. They have made Indian politics a matter of personal feud. Consequences have no terror for them; indeed, they do not occur to them until they happen. When they do happen, they either forget the cause, or if they remember it, they overlook it with a complacency which saves them from any remorse. They choose to stand on a pedestal of splendid isolation. They wall themselves off from their equals. They prefer to open themselves to their inferiors. They are very unhappy at and impatient of criticism, but are very happy to be fawned upon by flunkeys. Both have developed a wonderful stagecraft and arrange things in such a way that they are always in the limelight wherever they go. Each, of course, claims to be supreme. If supremacy were their only claim, it would be a small wonder.

In addition to supremacy, each claims infallibility for himself. Pius IX, during whose sacred regime as Pope the issue of infallibility was raging, said: "Before I was Pope, I believed in Papal infallibility, now I feel it." This is exactly the attitude of the two leaders whom Providence – may I say, in his unguarded moments – has appointed to lead us. This feeling of supremacy and infallibility is strengthened by the Press. One cannot help saying that.

The language used by Gardiner to describe the Northcliffe brand of journalism, in my opinion, quite appropriately describes the present state of journalism in India. Journalism in India was once a profession. It has now become a trade. It has no more moral function than the manufacture of soap. It does not regard itself as the responsible adviser of the public. To give the news uncoloured by any motive, to present a certain view of public policy which it believes to be for the good of the community, to correct and chastise without fear all those, no matter how high, who have chosen a wrong or a barren path, is not regarded by journalism in India its first or foremost duty. To accept a hero and worship him has become its principal duty. Under it, news gives place to sensation, reasoned opinion to unreasoning passion, appeal to the minds of responsible people to appeal to the emotions of the irresponsible. Lord Salisbury spoke of the Northcliffe journalism as written by office-boys for office-boys. Indian journalism is all that plus something more. It is written by drum-boys to glorify their heroes. Never has the interest of the country been sacrificed so senselessly for the propagation of hero-worship. Never has hero-worship become so blind as we see it in India today. There are, I am glad to say, honourable exceptions.

But they are too few, and their voice is never heard. Entrenched behind the plaudits of the Press, the spirit of domination exhibited by these two great men has transgressed all limits. By their domination, they have demoralised their followers and demoralised politics. By their domination, they have made half their followers fools and the other half hypocrites. In establishing their supremacy, they have taken the aid of "big business" and money magnates. For the first time in our country, money is taking the field as an organised power. The questions which President Roosevelt propounded for the American Public to consider will arise here, if they have not already arisen: Who shall rule – wealth or man? Which shall lead, money or intellect? Who shall fill public stations, educated and patriotic free men, or the feudal serfs of corporate capital? For the present, Indian politics, at any rate the Hindu part of it, instead of being spiritualized, has become grossly commercialised, so much so that it has become a byword for corruption. Many men of culture are refusing to concern themselves with this cesspool. Politics has become a kind of sewage system, intolerably unsavoury and unsanitary. To become a politician is like going to work in the drain.

Politics in the hands of these two great men has become a competition in extravaganza. If Mr. Gandhi is known as Mahatma, Mr. Jinnah must be known as Quaid-i-Azim. If Gandhi has the Congress, Mr. Jinnah must have the Muslim League. If the Congress has a Working Committee and the All-India Congress Committee, the Muslim League must have its Working Committee and its Council. The session of the Congress must be followed by a session of the League. If the Congress issues a statement, the League must also follow suit. If the Congress passes a Resolution of 17,000 words, the Muslim League's Resolution must exceed it by at least a thousand words. If the Congress President has a Press Conference, the Muslim League President must have his. If the Congress must address an appeal to the United Nations, the Muslim League must not allow itself to be outbidden. When is all this to end? When is there to be a settlement? There are no near prospects. They will not meet, except on preposterous conditions. Jinnah insists that Gandhi should admit that he is a Hindu. Gandhi insists that Jinnah should admit that he is one of the leaders of the Muslims. Never has there been such a deplorable state of bankruptcy of statesmanship as one sees in these two leaders of India. They are making long and interminable speeches, like lawyers whose trade it is to contest everything, concede nothing, and talk by the hour. Suggest anything by way of solution for the deadlock to either of them, and it is met by an everlasting "Nay." Neither will consider a solution to the problems which is not eternal. Between them, Indian politics has become "frozen," to use a well-known banking phrase, and no political action is possible.

How does Ranade strike us, as compared to these two? I have no personal impression to give. But reading what others have said, I think I can say what he must have been like. He had not a tinge of egotism in him. His intellectual attainments could have justified any amount of pride, nay, even insolence. But he was the most modest of men. Serious youths were captivated by his learning and geniality. Many, feeling completely under his sway, responded to his ennobling influence and moulded their whole lives with the passionate reverence for their adored master. He refused to be satisfied with the praises of fools and was never afraid of moving in the company of equals and of the give and take it involves. He never claimed to be a mystic relying on the inner voice. He was a rationalist, prepared to have his views tested in the light of reason and experience. His greatness was natural. He needed no aid of the stage, nor the technique of an assumed eccentricity, nor the means of a subsidised press. As I said, Ranade was principally a social reformer. He was not a politician in the sense of one who trades in politics. But he has played an important part in the political advancement of India. To some of the politicians, he acted as the teacher who secured such signal successes and who dazzled their critics by their brilliance. To some, he acted as the guide, but to all, he acted as the philosopher.

What was the political philosophy of Ranade? It may be summed up in three propositions:

(1) We must not set up as our ideal something which is purely imaginary. An ideal must be such that it must carry the assurance that it is a practicable one.

(2) In politics, the sentiment and temperament of the people are more important than intellect and theory. This is particularly so

in the matter of framing a constitution. A constitution is as much a matter of taste as clothes are. Both must fit, both must please.

(3) In political negotiations, the rule must be what is possible. That does not mean that we should be content with what is offered. No. It means that you must not refuse what is offered when you know that your sanctions are inadequate to compel your opponent to concede more.

These are the three main doctrines of Ranade's political philosophy. It would be quite easy to illustrate them by appropriate quotations from his writings and his speeches. There is no time for that, nor is there any necessity, for they must be clear to every student of Ranade's speeches and writings. Who could quarrel with Ranade on these three propositions, and if there be one, on which? On the first, only a visionary will quarrel. We need not take any notice of him. The second proposition is so evident that we could only ignore it at our peril. The third proposition is something on which a difference of opinion is possible. Indeed, it is this which divided the liberals from the Congressmen. I am not a Liberal, but I am sure the view Ranade held was the right one. There can be no compromise on principle, and there should not be. But once the principle is agreed upon, there can be no objection to realising it by instalments. Graduation in politics is inevitable, and when the principle is accepted, it is not harmful and indeed it may in certain circumstances be quite advantageous. On this third proposition, there was really no difference between him and Tilak, except this: Tilak would have the possible maximised by the application of sanctions; Ranade would look askance at sanctions. This is all. On the rest, they were agreed. The absence of sanctions in Ranade's political philosophy need not detract much from its worth. We all know what sanctions are available to us. We have tried all, old as well as new, with what effect I need not stop to describe.

## VIII

In celebrating the birthday of Ranade, we must not overlook what the critics and opponents are likely to say. The critics will ask what the point is in celebrating the birthday of Ranade. That the days of hero-worship are gone long past will be the line of their argument. The opponents will say, if I condemn idolatry when it pertains to Mr. Gandhi and to Mr. Jinnah, how do I join in idolising Mr. Ranade? These are very pertinent questions. True hero-worship is dying. Of that there is no doubt. It was dying even in the days of Carlyle, who indignantly complained against his age, saying:

"This is an age that, as it were, denies the existence of great men: denies the inevitableness of great men."

"Show our critics a great man," he said, and, "They begin to what they call 'account for him'; not to worship him but take the dimensions of him."

But hero-worship is certainly not dead in India. India is still, par excellence, the land of idolatry. There is idolatry in religion, there is idolatry in politics. Heroes and hero-worship is a hard, if unfortunate, fact in India's political life. I agree that hero-worship is demoralising for the devotee and dangerous to the country. I welcome the criticism, insofar as it conveys a caution that you must know that your man is really great before you start worshipping him. This, unfortunately, is not an easy task. For in these days, with the Press in hand, it is easy to manufacture great men. Carlyle used a happy phrase when he described the great men of history as so many banknotes. Like banknotes, they represent gold. What we have to see is that they are not forged notes. I admit that we ought to be more cautious in our worship of great men. For in this country, we have perhaps arrived at such a stage when, alongside the notice boards saying "beware of pickpockets," we need to have notice boards saying "beware of great men." Even Carlyle, who defended the worship of great men, warned his readers how:

"Multitudes of men have figured in history as great men who were false and selfish." He regretted deeply that "The world's wages (of homage) are pocketed (by these so-called great men), the world's work is not done. Heroes have gone out; quacks have come in."

Ranade never received the honours of apotheosis as these great men of India today are destined to receive. How could he? He did not come with a message hot from Senai. He performed no miracles and promised no speedy deliverance and splendour. He was not a genius, and he had no superhuman qualities. But there are compensations. If Ranade did not show splendour and dominance, he brought us no catastrophe. If he had no superhuman qualities to use in the service of India, India was saved from ruin by its abuse. If he was not a genius, he did not display that perverse super-subtlety of intellect and a temper of mind which is fundamentally dishonest and which has sown the seeds of distrust and which has made settlement so difficult of achievement. There is nothing exuberant and extravagant in Ranade. He refused to reap cheap notoriety by playing the part of an extremist. He refused to mislead people by playing upon and exploiting the patriotic sentiments of the people. He refused to be a party to methods which are crude, which have volume but no effect, and which are neither fool-proof nor knave-proof and which break the back even of the most earnest and sincere servants of the country and disable them from further effort. In short, Ranade was like the wise captain who knows that his duty is not to play with his ship clever and masterful tricks, just for effect and show in the midst of the ocean, but to take it safely to its appointed port. In short, Ranade was not a forged banknote and, in worshipping him, we have no feeling of kneeling before anything that is false.

In the second place, this celebration of Ranade's birthday is not all an act of hero-worship. Hero-worship in the sense of expressing our unbounded admiration is one thing. To obey the hero is a totally different kind of hero-worship. There is nothing wrong with the former, while the latter is no doubt a most pernicious thing. The former is only man's respect for everything which is noble and of which the great man is only an embodiment. The latter is the villain's fealty to his lord. The former is consistent with respect, but the latter is a sign of debasement. The former does not take away one's intelligence to think and independence to act. The latter makes one a perfect fool. The former involves no disaster to the State. The latter is the source of positive danger to it. In short, in celebrating Ranade's birthday we are not worshipping a boss who is elected by no one, accountable to no one and removable by no one, but paying our tribute of admiration to a leader who led and did not drive people, who sought to give effect to their deliberate judgement and did not try to impose his own will upon them by trickery or by violence.

In the third place, it is not for hero-worship for which this gathering has assembled. This is an occasion to remind ourselves of the political philosophy of Ranade. To my mind, it has become necessary to remind ourselves of it from time to time. For his is a philosophy which is safe and sound, sure if slow. Even if it does not glitter, it is nonetheless gold. Do any have doubts? If they have, let them ponder over the following utterances of Bismarck, Balfour and Morley. Bismarck, the great German Statesman, said:

"Politics is the game of the possible.".

Balfour, in his Introduction to Walter Bagehot's well-known book on the English Constitution, says:

"If we would find the true basis of the long drawn process which has gradually converted medieval monarchy into a modern democracy, the process by which so much has been changed and so little destroyed, we must study temperament and character rather than intellect and theory. This is a truth which those who recommend the wholesale adoption of British institutions in strange lands might remember with advantage. Such an experiment can hardly be without its dangers. Constitutions are easily copied; temperaments are not; and if it should happen that the borrowed constitution and the native temperament fail to correspond, the misfit may have serious results. It matters little what other gifts a people may possess if they are wanting in these which, from this point of view, are of most importance.

"If, for example, they have no capacity for grading their loyalties as well as for being moved by them; if they have no natural inclination to liberty and no natural respect for law; if they lack good humour and tolerate foul play; if they know not how to compromise or when; if they have not that distrust of extreme conclusions which is sometimes misdescribed as want of logic; if corruption does not repel them; and if their divisions tend to be either too numerous or too profound, the successful working of British institutions may be difficult or impossible. It may indeed be least possible where the arts of parliamentary persuasion and the dexterities of party management are brought to their highest perfection."

Morley has observed:

"To hurry on after logical perfection is to show one's ignorance of the material of that social structure with which the politician has to deal. To disdain anything short of an organic change in thought or institution is infatuation. To be willing to make such changes too frequently, even when they are possible, is foolhardiness. That fatal French saying about small reforms being the worst enemies of great reforms is, in the sense in which it is commonly used, a formula of social ruin."

These are the principles on which success in politics depends. Are they different from those which Ranade enunciated? It bespeaks greatness in Ranade that he should have propounded them years before Bismarck, Balfour and Morley.

The generation which Ranade served was wise in taking him as its political guide, friend and philosopher. His greatness lies in the fact that he can be a guide, friend and philosopher to this present, nay even to future generations.

There is one charge against Ranade which is frequently made and which I think must be met. It is said of Ranade that he believed that the conquest of India by the British was Providential, that it was in the best interest of India, that she should remain within the British Empire and that therein lay her final destiny. In short, Ranade is accused of being opposed to India's Independence.

The charge is founded on the following utterances of Ranade:

"It cannot be easily assumed that in God's Providence, such vast multitudes as those who inhabit India were placed centuries together under influences and restraints of alien domination, unless such influences and restraints were calculated to do lasting service in the building up of the strength and character of the people in directions in which the Indian races were most deficient. Of one thing we are certain, that after lasting over five hundred years, the Mohammedan Empire gave way and made room for the re-establishment of the old native races in the Punjab, and throughout Central Hindusthan and Southern India, on foundations of a much more solid character than those which yielded so easily before the assaults of the early Mohammedan conquerors.

"Both Hindus and Mohammedans lack many of those virtues represented by the love of order and regulated authority. Both are wanting in the love of municipal freedom, in the exercise of virtues necessary for civic life and in aptitudes for mechanical skill, in the love of science and research, in the love and daring of adventurous discovery, the resolution to master difficulties and in chivalrous respect for womankind. Neither the old Hindus nor the old Mohammedan civilisation was in a condition to train these virtues in a way to bring up the races of India on a level with those of Western Europe, and so the work of education had to be renewed, and it has been now going on for the past century and more under the Pax Brittanica with results – which all of us are witnesses to in ourselves."

A mere glance at these statements is enough to show that the charge is based on a misunderstanding, if not on a misreading, of the statements. The statements are plain and simple, and they cannot, even by inference, be said to lead to the conclusion that Ranade was opposed to India's independence. In that sense, the charge is false and without foundation.

These statements of Ranade, far from casting any reflection upon his self-respect, testify to his wisdom and to his sagacity. What did Ranade want to convey by these statements? As I understand them, I think Ranade wanted to convey two things. The first thing he wanted to convey was that the conquest of India by Britain has given India the time, the opportunity and the necessary shelter for rebuilding, renovating and repairing her economic and social structure, to refit herself for bearing the strain of any foreign aggression when she does become free. The second thing Ranade wanted to convey was that going out of the British Empire by India before she had satisfied and solidified herself into a single nation, unified in thought, in feeling and charged with a sense of a common destiny was to invite chaos and disruption in the name of independence.

How very important these truths are! People do not realise the part that shelter plays in the smooth working out of social, economic and political conflicts, which are inevitable in every society which desires to advance. The Late Prof. Maitland was once asked to explain why parliamentary institutions flourished in England but failed to take root in Europe. His answer reveals the importance of shelter. He said the difference was due to the English Channel. By this answer, what he meant to convey was that by reason of the English Channel, England was immune from foreign aggression while she was repairing her own body politic, and therefore, it became safe for people to fight against their King for liberty and also safe for the King to allow it to his people. This importance of shelter was also emphasised by Abraham Lincoln. In a speech devoted to showing why American political institutions were destined to remain perpetual, Lincoln said:

"All the armies of Europe, Asia and Africa combined... with a Bonaparte for a Commander, could not by force take a drink from Ohio, or make a track on the Blue Ridge in a trial of a thousand years."

In this, Lincoln was also emphasising the importance and the necessity of shelter for social reconstruction. India is not a sheltered country as England and America are. She lies across and on the roads, whether the roads are land routes, sea routes or air routes. As she has no shelter, the fear is that she will be broken up if she is attacked from outside while she is engaged in refitting herself. India needs a dry dock as a shelter for the period of her refitting, and the British Empire is a dry dock for her. Who can say that Ranade was not wise in asking his countrymen to bear in mind the importance of a shelter which the British Empire can give and which India needs so much?

A servient nation is always eager to cut the knot and declare its independence from the dominant nation. But it seldom stops to consider the effect of independence on itself. Such a consideration is, however, very important. It is not often realised that the knot which binds the servient nation to the dominant nation is more necessary to the servient nation than to the dominant nation. It depends upon the conditions inside the servient nation. The servient nation may be one whole. The servient nation may consist of parts. The parts may be such that they will never become one whole. Or the parts may be such that they are not yet one whole, but if held together longer, they will become one whole. The effect which the cutting of the knot will have on the servient nation will depend upon the internal condition of the servient nation. There may be every good in cutting the knot by a servient nation which is one whole. Nothing good or nothing worse can happen – depends upon how one looks at it – by the cutting of the knot by a nation in which the parts can never become one whole. But there is positive danger in the third case. The premature cutting of the knot is sure to lead to disintegration, where integration is desirable and possible. It would be a wanton act. This is the second danger which Ranade wanted to caution his countrymen against.

Who can say that Ranade was not wise in giving this caution? Those who are inclined to question its necessity have only to look to China. It has been 30 years since the Chinese Revolution took place. Have the Chinese settled down? No. People are still asking, "When will the Chinese revolution stop revolving?" and those who know the conditions in China cannot do better than say, "Perhaps in another hundred years." Has China found a stable government having the allegiance of all Chinese? Far from it. Indeed, if truth be told, China after the revolution has been a land of disunity and disruption, far more than she was ever before. The Revolution has produced a chaos of such magnitude that her very independence has been put in peril. Few Indians are aware of the fact that if China has not lost her independence as a result of the chaos caused by the Revolution, it is only because she had too many enemies who could not agree as to which of them should devour her. The Chinese Revolution was a great mistake. That was the opinion of Yuan Shih-k'ai, who said:

"I doubt whether the people of China are at present ripe for a Republic or whether under present conditions a Republic is adapted to the Chinese people... The adoption of a limited monarchy would bring conditions back to the normal and would bring stability much more rapidly than that end could be attained through any experimental form of government unsuited to the genius of the people or to the present conditions in China... My only reason for favouring the retention of the present Emperor is that I believe in a constitutional monarchy. If we are to have that form of government, there is nobody else whom the people would agree upon for his place. My sole aim, in this crisis, is to save China from dissolution and the many evils that would follow."

Those who think that China should be rather a warning to Indians than an example will, far from accusing Ranade for opposing India's independence, will be happy that he had the wisdom to foresee the evils of a premature revolution and warn his countrymen against taking a similar step.

## IX

Posterity is always interested in the last words and last regrets of great men. The last words of great men are not always significant of their experience of this world or their vision of the next. For instance, the last thoughts of Socrates were to call Crito and say, "We owe a cock to Aesculapius; discharge the debt, and by no means omit it." But their last regrets are always significant and worth pondering over.

Take the case of Napoleon. Napoleon, before his death at St Helena, showed evidence of being uneasy over three capital points which constituted his last regrets. They were that he could not have died at some supreme moment of his career; that he left Egypt and gave up his Eastern ambitions; and last but by no means the least, his defeat at Waterloo. Had Ranade any supreme regrets? One thing is certain that Ranade, if he had any, could not have had the same regrets such as those which disturbed the peace of mind of Napoleon. Ranade lived for service and not for glory. It mattered very little to him whether the moment of his death was glorious or inglorious, or whether he died as a hero, as a conqueror or a master, or whether he died as a common man, sometimes does of a common cold. As a matter of fact, Ranade was not troubled by any regrets. So far as the record goes, Ranade does not seem to be conscious of any act or event about which he had any regrets. He died a happy and peaceful death. But it is worthwhile asking, could Ranade have any regrets if he were to come to life today? I am sure there is one matter over which he will feel extremely grieved – namely, the present condition of the Liberal Party in India.

What is the present position of the Liberal Party in India? The Liberal Party is a casualty. Indeed, this is a very mild expression. The liberals are "the contemptibles" of Indian politics. To use the language Norton used in another connection, they are disowned by the people, unowned by the government, having the virtues of neither, but possessing the vices of both. There was a time when the Liberal Party was the rival of the Congress. Today, the relation of the Liberal Party to the Congress is that of a dog to his master. Occasionally, the dog barks at his master, but for most part of his life, he is content to follow him. What is the Liberal Party if not the tail of the Congress? Many are asking, why don't the liberals merge in the Congress – so useless has their existence become. How can Ranade help not regret the collapse of the Liberal Party? How can any Indian help regretting it?

The collapse of the Liberal Party is a tragedy for the liberals. But it is really a disaster for the country. The existence of a party is so essential to a popular government that it is impossible to conceive the possibility of getting on without it. As an eminent American historian says:

"It is easier to imagine the demolition of any part of our constitutional organisation, the submersion of a large part of what the constitution describes, than to imagine our getting on without political combinations: they are our vital institutions."

Indeed, to attempt to govern a country by the mass of voters without the control and discipline of a party is, to use the language of James Bryce:

"Like attempting to manage a rail-board by the votes of uninformed shareholders, or to lay the course of a sailing ship by the votes of the passengers."

It is undeniable that a party is an essential adjunct to popular government. But it is equally undeniable that the rule of a single party is fatal to popular government. In fact, it is a negation of popular government. The case of Germany and Italy furnishes the most cogent evidence on this point. Instead of taking a warning from the totalitarian States, we are taking them as models to copy. The one-party system is being hailed in this country in the name of national solidarity. Those who are doing so are failing to take note of the possibilities of tyranny, as well as the possibilities of misdirection of public affairs, which is inherent in the one-party government. To have a popular government run by a single party is to let democracy become a mere form, for despotism to play its part from behind it.

How, under one-party government, the tyranny of the majority ceases to be an empty phrase and becomes a menacing fact has been our experience, in India, under the Congress regime. Were we not told by Mr. Rajagopalachari that the separation of the Executive and the Judiciary, which was necessary under the British, is no longer necessary? Does it not show the despot's taste for blood? Despotism does not cease to be despotism because it is elective. Nor does despotism become agreeable because the despots belong to our own kindred. To make it subject to election is no guarantee against despotism. The real guarantee against despotism is to confront it with the possibility of its dethronement, of its being laid low, of its being superseded by a rival party.

Every government is liable to error of judgement, a great many are liable to bad administration, and not a few to corruption, injustice and acts of oppression and bad faith. No government ought to be free from criticism. But who can criticise a government? Left to individuals, it can never be done. Sir Toby has left behind advice as to how one should deal with one's enemy. He said: "So soon as ever thou seest him, draw, and as thou drawest, swear horrible." But this is not possible for an individual who wants to stand up against a government. There are various things against individuals' successfully playing that part. There is in the first place what Bryce calls the fatalism of the multitude, that tendency to acquiesce and submit due to the sense of the insignificance of individual effort, the sense of helplessness arising from the belief that the affairs of men are swayed by large forces whose movements cannot be turned by individual effort. In the second place, there is the possibility of the tyranny of the majority, which often manifests itself in suppressing and subjecting to penalties and other social disabilities persons who do not follow the majority, of which some of us have good experience during the Congress regime. In the third place, there is the fear of the C.I.D., the Gestapo and all the other instrumentalities which are at the disposal of the government to shadow its critics and to silence them.

The secret of freedom is courage, and courage is born in the combination of individuals into a party. A party is necessary to run the government. But two parties are necessary to keep the government from despotism. A democratic government can remain democratic only if it is worked by two parties – a party in power and a party in opposition. As Jennings puts it:

"If there is no opposition, there is no democracy. 'His Majesty's Opposition' is no idle phrase. His Majesty needs an opposition as well as a government."

In the light of these considerations, who could deny them and say that the collapse of the Liberal Party in India is not a major disaster? Without the resuscitation of the Liberal Party or the formation of another party, the fight for freedom will result in loss of freedom, for despotism is antithetical to freedom, whether the despotism is native or foreign. It is a pity Indians have lost sight of this fact. But I have no doubt those who are shouting that the Congress is the only party and that the Congress is the nation will live to rue their decision.

Why has the Liberal Party collapsed? Is there something wrong with the philosophy of Ranade? Is there anything wrong with the men in the Liberal Party? Or is the working of the Liberal Party at fault? I, for one, hold that there is nothing fundamentally wrong with the philosophy of Ranade. Nor can it be said that of the two, the Congress has the best cause and the Liberal Party the best men. The Liberal Party has both. To my mind, what has brought about the collapse of the Liberal Party is the complete lack of organisation.

It may not be without interest to expose the weaknesses in the organisation of the Liberal Party.

As pointed out by Pendleton Herring in his volume on Politics of Democracy, the organisation of a party is spread over three concentric rings. The centre ring represents the oligarchy in control of the party organisation – what is called the High Command. There are associated with it its workers who are primarily concerned with securing their livelihood through the party organisation, whether as party officials or through public office. They are called professional politicians and constitute the party machine. Surrounding this inner group – the High Command and the machine – there is a large circle of persons bound to the party by ties of tradition and emotional loyalty. They think of the principles professed by the party. They are more concerned with its ideals and symbols than with the acts of the professional party workers and leaders. They vote for the party's ideal rather than for the party's record.

Outside this second ring lies that vast body of people who are not attached to any party. It is a floating population. The reason for their being unattached is either because they are aimless, thoughtless, or because they have particular interests which are not included in the platform of any party. Those outside the second ring constitute the most vital field of action for a political party. They are the prize which a party must capture. To capture this prize, it is not enough to enunciate principles and formulate policies. Men are not interested in principles and policies. But they are interested in accomplishing things. What is necessary for a party is to bring about concerted action. For in the words of President Woodrow Wilson, given self-government with majority rule, things can be accomplished not by individual voice but by concerted action.

Now, for concerted action, what is necessary is the crystallisation of individual opinions into public opinion. This crystallisation or building up of public opinion as a sanction behind a particular principle becomes the main function of a party. Theoretically, political parties are agencies for the expression and execution of public opinion; but in practice, parties create, direct, influence and often control public opinion. Indeed, this is the chief function of a party. For this, a party must do two things. In the first place, it must establish contact with the masses. It must go out among the masses with its wares – its principles, policies, ideas and candidates. In the second place, it must carry on propaganda among the masses in favour of its wares. It must animate them and enlighten them, to quote Bryce again, "give the voters some knowledge of the political issues they have to decide, to inform them of their leaders and the crimes of their opponents." These are the basic factors from which concerted action can arise. A party which fails to forge concerted action has no right to call itself a party.

Which of these things has the Liberal Party done as an organisation? The Liberal Party has only the High Command. It has no machine. Not having any machine, the high command is only a shadow. Its following is confined to that second concentric ring consisting of persons who are bound by ties of tradition. The leaders have nothing to evoke emotional loyalty. They have no war cry to gather a crowd. The Liberal Party does not believe in mass contact. It would be difficult to imagine a party so completely isolated and insulated from the main mass of people. It does not believe in conversion. Not that it has no Gospel to preach; but like the Hindu religion, it is a nonproselytising creed. It believes in the formulation of principles and policies. But it does not work for giving effect to them. Propaganda and concerted action are anathema to the Liberal Party. Individual voices and annual meetings and clamour for invitation when a Cripps arrives or when the Viceroy decides to invite important individuals, have become the limits of its political activity. Is there any wonder that the Liberal Party has fallen into disrepute? The Liberal Party has forgotten the most elementary fact that organisation is essential for the accomplishment of any purpose and, particularly in politics, where the harnessing of so many divergent elements in a working unity is so great.

Who is responsible for this collapse of the Liberal Party in India? However much we may regret to have to say it, I think it will have to be admitted that the responsibility for this catastrophe does, to some extent, fall on Ranade. Ranade belonged to the upper classes. He was born and bred among them. He never became a man of the masses. The Liberal Party has no machine, and the reason why it did not forge a machine is because it did not believe in mass contact. This aversion to mass contact is the legacy of Ranade. In avoiding mass contact, the party is following the tradition left by Ranade. There is another legacy of Ranade to the Liberal Party and that relates to the false faith in the driving force of principles and policies. Mazzini once said, "You may kill men, you cannot kill a great idea." To me, it appears to be a most mistaken view. Men are mortal. So are ideas. It is wrong to hold that an idea will take root proprio vigore. An idea needs propagation as much as a plant needs watering. Both will otherwise wither and die. Ranade agreed with Mazzini and did not believe that the fructification of an idea needed the resources of strenuous husbandry. If the Liberal Party is content with mere formulation of principles and policies, it is also because of this tradition of Ranade.

What is the duty of the liberals? All liberals I know will say, our duty is to follow the master. What else could be the attitude of a devout band of disciples? But can anything be more mistaken or more uncritical? Such an attitude implies two things. It means that a great man works by imposing his maxims on his disciples. It means that the disciples should not be wiser than the master. Both of these conclusions are wrong. They do injustice to the master. No great man really does his work by crippling his disciple by forcing on them his maxims or his conclusions. What a great man does is not to impose his maxims on his disciples. What he does is to evoke them, to awaken them to a vigorous and various exertion of their faculties. Again, the pupil only takes his guidance from his master. He is not bound to accept his master's conclusions. There is no ingratitude in the disciple not accepting the maxims or the conclusions of his master. For even when he rejects them, he is bound to acknowledge to his master in deep reverence: "You awakened me to be myself; for that I thank you." The master is not entitled to less. The disciple is not bound to give more.

It is, therefore, a wrong to the master as well as to himself for the disciple to bind himself to the maxims and conclusions of his master. His duty is to know the principles and, if he is convinced of their value and their worth, to spread them. That is the wish of every master. Jesus wished it, Buddha wished it. I am sure the same must be the wish of Ranade. It follows that if the liberals have faith in and love and respect for Ranade, their supreme duty lies not merely in assembling together to sing his praises, but in organising themselves for spreading the gospel of Ranade.

What hope is there of the liberals coming forward to fulfil this duty? Signs are very depressing. In the last election, the liberals did not even contest the seats. That, of course, is in itself a matter of some surprise. But this pales into nothing when one recalls the announcement made by the Rt. Honourable Srinivas Shastri – the Leading Light of the Liberal Party – that he wished the Congress to succeed!! There is no parallel to this except in the treacherous and treasonous conduct of Bhishma, who lived on the bounty of the

Kauravas but wished and worked for the success of their enemies, the Pandavas. This shows even the liberals had lost faith in the gospel of Ranade. If this is the general condition of health of the Liberal Party, it is better if the party died. It would clear the way for a new orientation, and spare us the tedium of the idle clatter of liberals and liberalism. For such an event, even Ranade may express satisfaction from his grave.

# About the Author

Dr. B. R. Ambedkar was the Chief Architect of the Indian Constitution and independent India's first Minister of Law and Justice. Famously called Babasaheb Ambedkar, he was born on 14th April 1891 in the military cantonment of Mhow, Madhya Pradesh, as the 14th and last child of Ramji Maloji Sakpal and Bhimabai Sakpal. After completing his studies at Elphinstone College, Ambedkar earned his Doctorate Degree in Economics from Columbia University and the University of London. Some of B. R. Ambedkar's famous works include *Castes in India: Their Mechanism, Genesis and Development; The Evolution of Provincial Finance in British India; Pakistan or The Partition of India; and Riddles in Hinduism.*